THE BEST OF CANADA'S NEW WRITERS

THE JOURNEY PRIZE

STORIES

SELECTED BY
ALEXANDER **MacLEOD**
ALISON **PICK**
SARAH **SELECKY**

EMBLEM
McClelland & Stewart

Emblem is an imprint of McClelland & Stewart Ltd.
Emblem and colophon are registered trademarks of McClelland & Stewart Ltd.

A cataloguing record for this publication is available from Library and Archives Canada.

We acknowledge the financial support of the Government of Canada through the Book Publishing Industry Development Program and that of the Government of Ontario through the Ontario Media Development Corporation's Ontario Book Initiative. We further acknowledge the support of the Canada Council for the Arts and the Ontario Arts Council for our publishing program.

Published simultaneously in the United States of America by McClelland & Stewart Ltd., P.O. Box 1030, Plattsburgh, New York 12901

Library of Congress Control Number: 2011932523

Cover art: Dreamstime

Typeset in Janson by M&S, Toronto
Printed and bound in Canada

McClelland & Stewart Ltd.
75 Sherbourne Street
Toronto, Ontario
M5A 2P9
www.mcclelland.com

2 3 4 5 15 14 13 12

THE JOURNEY PRIZE

STORIES

WINNERS OF THE $10,000 JOURNEY PRIZE

1989
Holley Rubinsky for
"Rapid Transits"

1990
Cynthia Flood for "My Father
Took a Cake to France"

1991
Yann Martel for "The Facts
Behind the Helsinki Roccamatios"

1992
Rozena Maart for "No Rosa,
No District Six"

1993
Gayla Reid for
"Sister Doyle's Men"

1994
Melissa Hardy for
"Long Man the River"

1995
Kathryn Woodward for "Of
Marranos and Gilded Angels"

1996
Elyse Gasco for "Can You Wave
Bye Bye, Baby?"

1997 (shared)
Gabriella Goliger for
"Maladies of the Inner Ear"

Anne Simpson for
"Dreaming Snow"

1998
John Brooke for
"The Finer Points of Apples"

1999
Alissa York for "The Back of the
Bear's Mouth"

2000
Timothy Taylor for
"Doves of Townsend"

2001
Kevin Armstrong for
"The Cane Field"

2002
Jocelyn Brown for
"Miss Canada"

2003
Jessica Grant for
"My Husband's Jump"

2004
Devin Krukoff for
"The Last Spark"

2005
Matt Shaw for "Matchbook for a
Mother's Hair"

2006
Heather Birrell for
"BriannaSusannaAlana"

2007
Craig Boyko for
"OZY"

2008
Saleema Nawaz for
"My Three Girls"

2009
Yasuko Thanh for
"Floating Like the Dead"

2010
Devon Code for
"Uncle Oscar"

ABOUT THE JOURNEY PRIZE STORIES

The $10,000 Journey Prize is awarded annually to an emerging writer of distinction. This award, now in its twenty-third year, and given for the eleventh time in association with the Writers' Trust of Canada as the Writers' Trust of Canada/McClelland & Stewart Journey Prize, is made possible by James A. Michener's generous donation of his Canadian royalty earnings from his novel *Journey*, published by McClelland & Stewart in 1988. The Journey Prize itself is the most significant monetary award given in Canada to a developing writer for a short story or excerpt from a fiction work in progress. The winner of this year's Journey Prize will be selected from among the ten stories in this book.

The Journey Prize Stories has established itself as the most prestigious annual fiction anthology in the country, introducing readers to the finest new literary writers from coast to coast for more than two decades. It has become a who's who of up-and-coming writers, and many of the authors who have appeared in the anthology's pages have gone on to distinguish themselves with collections of short stories, novels, and literary awards. The anthology comprises a selection from submissions made by the editors of literary journals from across the country, who have chosen what, in their view, is the most exciting writing in English that they have published in the previous year. In recognition of the vital role journals play in fostering literary voices, McClelland & Stewart makes its own award of

$2,000 to the journal that originally published and submitted the winning entry.

This year the selection jury comprised three acclaimed writers:

Alexander MacLeod's debut collection, *Light Lifting*, was a finalist for the Scotiabank Giller Prize, the Danuta Gleed Award, two Atlantic Book Awards, a regional Commonwealth Writers' Prize for Best First Book, and the Frank O'Connor International Short Story Award. A previous contributor to *The Journey Prize Stories*, Alexander holds degrees from the University of Windsor, the University of Notre Dame, and McGill University. He lives in Dartmouth, Nova Scotia, and teaches at Saint Mary's University in Halifax.

Alison Pick is the author of two novels, *The Sweet Edge* and *Far to Go*, winner of the 2010 Canadian Jewish Book Award for Fiction, and two books of poetry. She was the winner of the 2005 CBC Literary Award for Poetry and the 2002 Bronwen Wallace for most promising writer under the age of thirty-five. Currently on Faculty at the Humber School for Writers Correspondence Program, she lives with her family in Toronto. For more information, please visit www.alisonpick.com.

Sarah Selecky's debut collection, *This Cake Is for the Party*, was a finalist for the Scotiabank Giller Prize and a regional Commonwealth Writers' Prize for Best First Book, and longlisted for the Frank O'Connor International Short Story Award. A previous contributor to *The Journey Prize Stories*, Sarah earned her MFA in Creative Writing at the University of British Columbia and has been teaching creative writing in her living room for the past ten years. She lives in Toronto. For more information, please visit www.sarahselecky.ca.

The jury read a total of eighty-five submissions without knowing the names of the authors or those of the journals in which the stories originally appeared. McClelland & Stewart would like to thank the jury for their efforts in selecting this year's anthology and, ultimately, the winner of this year's Journey Prize.

McClelland & Stewart would also like to acknowledge the continuing enthusiastic support of writers, literary journal editors, and the public in the common celebration of new voices in Canadian fiction.

For more information about *The Journey Prize Stories*, please consult our website: www.mcclelland.com/jps.

CONTENTS

INTRODUCTION

This is a short book. A harmless-looking thing. Feel the easy weight of it in your hands, its modest heft. What could such a slim volume possibly contain? A book this small could slip into the back pocket of your jeans and still leave room for gum. It could bang around at the bottom of your knapsack and you'd never notice. Or it could just sit there for a few weeks, quiet and still, in the stack beside your bed. But don't get too comfortable with it. This little book holds ten of the best short stories published in Canada this year, and it introduces you to ten of the most exciting new writers in this country. You can almost feel the potential trembling inside. Where are these new artists going to take us? Who are we going to meet along the way? How much can they achieve with the short story form? Crack the spine of this skinny little book if you want to find out.

Although we enjoyed putting this collection together, it didn't turn out exactly the way we planned. When we first started this process, we thought we'd be making a bigger book: something . . . busier. We thought it might work like one of those British roundabouts, a circular point of intersection where many different vehicles travelling along many different routes converge at the same time. We thought our anthology might be able to bring a variety of elements together, coordinate them, and synchronize all this wildly varied movement into one perfect loop where each story maintains its own autonomy while simultaneously contributing to the efficient function and form of the whole.

Think of it: such happy comingling, such coordination and interdependence. Wouldn't it have been great if our book emerged with that kind of balance and precision? Wouldn't it have been great if we could have made everything fit together without any conflict or tension, without any sharp edges jutting out? Maybe, but that's not what happened here.

"Forget about good," wrote the designer Bruce Mau. "Good is a known quantity. Good is what we all agree on. As long as you stick to good, you'll never have real growth." In our deliberations, we searched for new growth in Canadian writing. Instead of the safest, smoothest work, we sought out arresting pieces that defied expectations and interrupted the flow, stories that made us stop and wonder, stories that showed us new ways of the seeing the world. We wanted to find sentences that excited us and stories that moved us. We wanted to feel changed in some way. And then we all had to agree on what that felt like.[1] Was that asking too much?

In the beginning, we independently read through a stack of almost one hundred stories – more online journal submissions than ever before, we were told – and then we emailed each other with our long lists of contenders. Overall, we were a compatible group of jurors. For the most part, our opinions overlapped. And yet! Despite our general agreement, there were some careful quarrels. In the end, it turns out that editing a literary anthology is not a job for peacekeepers. In this business, where

---

[1] We each chose a story or two that the other jurors didn't favour. To these stories, we say: *Know that you are loved.*

every aesthetic choice really matters, a testy scrap is always more valuable and interesting than tepid consensus. As we hope these selections will demonstrate, a good story needs conflict and tension and commitment. It needs to make us think and feel in powerful ways.

Several stories appeared on all three of our long lists, and though we often appreciated them for different reasons, not all of those first selections made it through to the book. On the other hand, there were some stories that appeared on only one or two of the opening lists. When we looked at them again, though, they gained more support as we moved through our deliberations, and some of those initial outliers eventually made the final cut.

Often we felt that a story was close, almost perfect, but lacking in one essential element or another. And so many of the submitted stories felt the same. So it was tempting to choose the innovative stories first. We wanted to reward these audacious, deviant stories. We loved that they were brave enough to find new ground, that they broke out of that claustrophobic Canadian Prose terrarium. "But the author tried something different," we'd say as we presented our case. The response, inevitably, was: "Okay, but did they succeed?" Then we'd put on our teaching glasses, peer at the page, and talk about how we'd have edited it if given the chance.

It was also tempting to choose stories that were competent and well-delivered. They didn't give off light, perhaps, but they had been edited and polished to a satisfactory shine. Most of the stories in the stack were solid in this way. But when we were pressed to defend them, to really get behind them and explain why we loved them, we had to admit we had chosen them because we couldn't find anything wrong with them. And that was not good enough.

When it came time to make our lists, we agreed on almost everything. Almost. On the toughest choices, we stated our cases and argued for and against. For the stalemates, we agreed to disagree, and then we voted and stood behind those decisions. Nobody got everything they wanted, and nobody got completely shut out. It worked the way it should, and we produced a book that accurately reflects the shared and sometimes conflicted vision of our group. Ultimately, there were only a small number of stories that lifted us out of our world and kept us there, aloft. So we agreed that we'd rather be more selective in choosing the contents of the anthology this year, and showcase those standout stories. That was the biggest surprise, the end result of all our reading. Out of the whole stack, out of almost one hundred stories from all across the country, we could only find and agree on ten.

There are advantages to being this selective, though. In previous introductions to *The Journey Prize Stories*, the jurors could usually only gesture toward the book that follows. When space is tight, they have to pick and choose, and be strategic about which stories will get a little extra attention, a few intriguing lines to whet the reader's appetite. In our case, we have plenty of room, and since we stand behind all these pieces, we decided to give each one a few precise words of praise.

Seyward Goodhand's "The Fur Trader's Daughter" is a good place to start. This story bewitched us with its weird steampunk magic and sentences to swoon over. It is a kind of postmodern fairy tale we've never quite seen before. Goodhand has written a world studded with incongruities and anachronisms, a time that is neither entirely the past nor entirely the present, a story that captivates us because it is both utterly weird and dangerously familiar.

Moving from the postmodern to the ancient, Ross Klatte's "First-Calf Heifer" reads initially like a story plucked from deep in the archives of Canadian fiction. Klatte works with some powerful raw materials in this piece: light and dark, life and death, innocence and experience, fathers and sons. This story of one day and night on a cattle farm brings us through opposing rites of tenderness and terror, and is structured around one pure and visceral scene that sticks in the reader's mind and refuses to go away.

We appreciated the subtle restraint of Michele Serwatuk's "My Eyes Are Dim." Her detailed description of the days after an earthquake is clear and unmediated, conspicuously precise and composed. When you read it, you feel that the sentences themselves have become the very consciousness of the narrator: she is in shock.

When we read Jay Brown's description of making ice on cobblestone laneways – "The ice accumulated like tree rings, each blanketing the other with surety and fastness – a molecular perfection" – we knew we had stumbled upon gold. "The Girl from the War" is written with skilful and striking narration. It is also paced exceptionally, right up to its astonishing finish.

Beautiful pacing and writing also characterize "Toupée" by Michelle Winters. The first sentence alerted us that we had found something fresh: "I saw him on the subway for the first time the day I brought the meat bomb to work." But the most moving part of this story about a disgruntled employee is the exquisite and powerful turn in the last line of dialogue; the deft use of a sad refrain made us wince (in a good way).

Similarly, the narrator in "What I Would Say," a sassy, clever monologue by Jessica Westhead, produced both laughter and cringing. In six short pages, Westhead manages to draw her protagonist in her flawed entirety. She seems eerily familiar, reminding us of other people we've known and of the darker, unacknowledged side of ourselves.

The protagonist in Fran Kimmel's "Laundry Day" had us rooting for her as she struggled against difficult odds. An evocative and deceptively simple story, "Laundry Day" is packed with vivid, visceral details. The pacing and tension are also excellent, culminating in a big exhale at the story's conclusion.

The main character in "The Extra" by Michael Christie is likewise disenfranchised. An unreliable narrator who is inevitably done wrong, he draws us immediately into his world. This story is heartbreaking and compelling all the way through: the ending packs a huge emotional punch. We expect to see more great things from Michael Christie in the future.

"The Dead Roads" by D.W. Wilson presents a cast of three vividly drawn characters hurtling through the Rocky Mountains at eighty miles an hour in a '67 Camaro. Their story teeters on the edge of those chasms that stretch between loyalty, friendship, and desire. Carried by the sometimes sad, sometimes elated voice of its narrator, this piece grapples with change and desperation and the ultimate selfishness of love.

Miranda Hill's "Petitions to Saint Chronic" focuses on a different kind of shared desperation, a different kind of worry, and ultimately, a different kind of faith. What does a true miracle look like? Can a man really fall from twenty-four storeys and live to tell the tale? Where should we place our belief and why? In this nuanced story, Hill's modern-day pilgrims keep vigil in a hospital waiting room, and we as readers stand right there with them, holding on for deliverance.

This is where we leave you now, waiting on the cusp of a reading experience that will reflect this particular moment in Canadian literature and our hope for its future. We understand that any jury process is flawed, and that another jury might have – would have – produced a different book. We have no doubt left some stories out that others would have included. So it goes. We trust, in the end, that good writing will eventually rise to the top, and that all these writers will get the recognition they deserve. This may be a little book, and it may only contain ten stories, but we think it's pretty damn good.

Alexander MacLeod
Alison Pick
Sarah Selecky
June 2011

THE **JOURNEY** PRIZE

STORIES

MICHAEL CHRISTIE

THE EXTRA

Me and Rick, we rent a basement suite at the bottom of Baldev's house. Actually, we only call it that to welfare so they'll give us the most amount of money for rent, but really it's just a basement, no suite part. The walls are 2x4s with cotton candy in between and there's no toilet or sink and it smells bad like your wrist when you leave your watch on too long. We sleep on hunks of foam beside the furnace between an orange lawnmower and used cans of paint that Baldev keeps down there. We take dumps at the gas station down the street and pee in plastic jugs we pour down a drain in the alley. Then at the tap on the side of the house, we rinse them and fill them for drinking and washing our pits and crotches. We used to have different jugs for peeing and drinking but then we got tired of remembering which was which.

When I say we rent, I really mean I do because my disability worker, Linda, sends a cheque for $500 a month to Baldev because she can't trust me with my money for the reason of my brain being disabled. But me and Rick and Baldev have this deal where Baldev gives us $200 of the rent back in cash as long as we don't complain about the basement and how it's just a basement.

Rick needs my help. He can't get welfare because years ago he got kicked off for not telling them he had a job while he was still getting cheques. But Rick says we're lucky because I have a disabled brain and we get more money than the regular welfare pays anyway, so it works out, and we split the disabled money right down the middle. Without Rick I'd be starving with flies buzzing on my face or back in a group home. He says what we're going to do with our money because I'm bad at numbers, and also he cooks me dinners and lunches on his hot plate. He sometimes cooks spaghetti or mostly different stews he gets out of a can. He always makes me wait until the stew is hot before we eat because I eat things cold because I'm bad at waiting. It's just more proper he says. Then he says it lasts longer in your belly if it's hot. When I ask why, he says because then your belly has to wait for it to get cool before it can soak it up.

Rick could have any job he wanted because he's sharp. He does our laundry and he made a copy of the key to the gas station bathroom and he gives himself homemade tattoos with a guitar string and gets really mad whenever he thinks somebody is ripping us off. Rick moved to Vancouver from Halifax but he never was a fisherman. He never set foot on a boat, he says, and besides there's more fish at your average pet store than in the whole goddamn ocean these days because of those big Japanese fish-vacuums he told me about. But he's not lazy. He's been a roofer, a car-parker, a painter, a tree planter, and he once worked nights mopping at a big twenty-four-hour hardware store. But now he just goes to WorkPower with me, which I'll tell you about later. He even used to be married but his wife left him because she was a rotten witch. She got everything, he says. Everything was his house and his kids and all his stuff that he bought with hard-earned money. He even had one of those trucks with four tires on the back. He talks about it sometimes when he's falling asleep after he's had some cans of the beer with lots of Xs all over it. Rick says I'm lucky I can't taste the beer. He named it swill, even though I can tell he likes it because it makes him a mix of confused and happy and tired.

Near the end of the month, when the disabled money and the money we get back from Baldev runs out, we get up at six in the morning. Then we put on our steeled-toe boots and bike to a place called WorkPower to stand in line to get jobs. Sometimes it's unloading boxes from trucks, or tearing copper wires out of buildings nobody wants. One time we had to carry blocks of ice from a truck to a freezer in a fish market and the gloves they gave us were thin as the butt of an old pair of underwear. Rick wanted to tell them where to stick it so bad but if one of the bosses complains to WorkPower they won't let us back. I like WorkPower because every time it's different but Rick doesn't like it because he thinks it's shit work. I ask him what shit work means and he says anything that makes you feel or look like shit.

One day after me and Rick got back from a whole day of picking up cigarette butts at a construction site, Baldev came down the stairs from his part of the house where at the top there is a door that doesn't lock on our side but does on Baldev's side. It's always locked, I've checked.

Rick asked Baldev who the hell he thought he was. He said, You can't just come down here without properly notifying us, it ain't legal.

Baldev nodded like he thought so too and said he had a thing to tell us.

Rick stuck his hands in his armpits and told him to go on and say it.

I am changing, Baldev said. My friends I cannot be able to give you this money-back deal in the future.

Rick got the vein in his forehead that he gets when he thinks he's getting ripped off. It's shaped like one of those sticks that finds water.

So sorry, Baldev said. This is because the property taxes that we have, they are going up.

Well what if the city finds out this here ain't exactly a legal suite? Rick said. But I didn't want Baldev to get in trouble for the basement, he has three or maybe four kids who I hear stomping around upstairs and he has a wife who cooks food that smells good in a way like no food I've ever ate. I told Baldev we wouldn't tell on him.

You must vacate if you are wishing, my friends, Baldev said, ignoring me and what I said. Then he went up the stairs and I heard the door lock.

Rick kicked some of our stuff around for a while but he wasn't that mad because when I told him everything was going to be okay, we'd just work a little harder, he started laughing. Then he said we'd have to go back to WorkPower every day this week if we wanted to eat. I told him I didn't mind shit work as long as my disability worker didn't find out I wasn't as disabled as I was supposed to be, that I could carry boxes and pick up cigarette butts, and then stop giving me my cheques. Rick said they wouldn't find out as long as I kept my mouth shut for the rest of the night. Then he rode his bike to go buy some beer with lots of Xs on it because he can't go to sleep early without at least a few.

The next day, we were in our steeled-toe boots on our way back from cutting weeds as high as our heads at a place that sells motor homes beside a highway. We had money in our pockets and we went to get some burgers because Rick said he was too damn tired to cook anything on the hot plate.

You eat your hamburgers too fast, Rick said, you can't even taste them. I told him I taste them good enough, but we both know I can't really taste anything too good because on account of my brain being disabled. But sometimes Rick acts like he's too much of the boss so I have to set him straight. If you're wondering why my brain is disabled it's because when I was born it didn't get enough air because there was some problem with my mom or the way I came out. My mom said they knew right after I came out because the doctor poked me on the feet with something but I didn't care. Then he put lights in my eyes but my eyes didn't really care either. The doctor just frowned, she said. Most of the time I forget it's damaged. Maybe it's too damaged to know it's damaged. Or maybe it's not damaged enough for me to notice. Either way it's not very bad.

Rick always leaves his burger wrappers and his tray on the table. He says he doesn't want to take away the people's jobs who clean up, but I throw his out for him because I think they'd still have jobs but just do less if everybody pitched in more. While I was at the garbage, a guy was talking to Rick. He had nice clothes like a disability worker and had one of those pocket telephones in his hand. He talked the same as Rick. Because Rick's from Halifax, he says burr or guiturr when he tries to say bar or guitar, but he can turn it off when he wants. He's really good at being me too, which is funny for a while then makes me mad if he acts too much like a retard because I'm not. Rick told the guy we were working in construction but I could see the guy looking at the long pieces of yellow grass still stuck in my hair. I got bored of their talking so I went to the bathroom and drank out of the tap.

When we rode our bikes home Rick said him and the guy had gone to high school together back in Halifax and the guy had gave Rick a card with his name on it and said he should call him if our construction jobs slow down because now he was working for the movies and they needed some extra people for a movie that they were making. It'd be a lot easier than WorkPower believe me, Rick said, but I didn't believe him because bad things always happened whenever Rick got happy about something.

In our basement he said he always thought he might be in the movies then he asked me to grab him another of the beers that we keep in a bucket of water outside so they're more cold. The rest of the night I had to listen to him practice talking normal, like not saying burr or guiturr. Then he put on the classic rock station, which is music that is older and everybody agrees is pretty good, while he did the kind of pushups where you do the clap in the middle or just go on your knuckles.

—

After waiting three days Rick called the guy from the payphone at the gas station where we take dumps. Rick came back and hugged me and said we were going to have a party because he had just got us both jobs as extras.

I asked him what extras were.

He said they were the people in movies who stood around in the background and made everything seem more real just by being there.

It seemed like something we'd be good at, but I was still worried. I'll do it, I told Rick, as long as I don't have to say anything because I can't talk or remember very good because of my brain being disabled and Rick said no problemo.

That night, during our party, Rick drank lots of beers and threw our steeled-toe boots out on the lawn. Then he went up the stairs and pounded on Baldev's door yelling about room service. I told him to stop because it was three in the morning and he'd wake the kids and they probably had to get up early and go to school. He did what I said and came back downstairs. He looked at his pictures of the rotten witch for a few minutes, then started sleeping.

The next day Rick said we needed some nice clothes because they wouldn't want to film us if we looked like shit.

I don't think we look like shit, I said, and I stuffed my hands into the pockets of my favorite orange hoodie that I was wearing because there was white parts on the sleeves from me wiping my nose on them.

We just have to make sure they don't think we're bums who don't deserve the job, he said, but luckily we saved some money for just this kind of occasion. Close your eyes.

Why, I said.

I'm making a withdrawal from our emergency fund, he said.

I faked shutting my eyes and saw him reach for the pineapple can he'd hid behind an old dartboard, which I already knew was there. He pulled out some money and put some back.

Okay, he said.

We biked along Cordova second-hand stores to get some clothes for our new job as extra people. Rick got a white shirt that was only a little yellow around the collar, some black pants, some shoes he called loafers, and some shades. I just wanted another hoodie, but he made me get some nice jeans and a T-shirt with a collar on it that had a little picture of a guy on a horse holding a sword in the air like he was going to kill somebody. In the change room, Rick switched the tags on them so they were only two bucks each. But the old lady was nice and didn't make us pay for them anyway.

The day came, which was good because Rick said we were out of money and we had to eat some donuts out of a dumpster on our way downtown to the movie place. When we got there, a woman made us wait in a room with a whole lot of other extra people, who were either reading magazines about movie stars or had their ears to their pocket telephones. Some were making appointments to be extra people for other movies and some were talking more quiet to their families and friends.

After a while, they took us into a big room with lots of clothes on racks where we waited some more. Then they brought our costumes. I took mine out of the plastic bag and didn't understand it. One of the clothes ladies had to help me put it on and I was embarrassed because she saw my underwear.

I put my golf shirt on a hanger and she hung it up. The costume was just bits of fur glued to this dirty net made out of canvas that hung off me like a bathrobe made out of a chewed-up dog. I also got these leather boots that were like moccasins, except they had these little blinking lights on them.

What the hell is this? I heard Rick ask the clothes lady when he got his, which was like mine but he had a helmet and these big black plastic horns coming out of the shoulders.

She talked with pins in her mouth and said it was his costume.

What kind of person wears rags and furs and horns and shredded-up leather? Rick said.

She said this is a movie that takes place in the future.

Rick wanted to know how in the hell that explained anything.

I hadn't been working in movies very long but I had already learned that when a movie person doesn't like what someone else is saying they just walk away from them, and that is exactly what the costume lady did, which made all shapes of veins bulge under Rick's helmet.

After everybody was dressed up they took us back to the waiting room.

How do you think they know what people are going to look like in the future? I asked Rick who was reading one of the movie star magazines.

Maybe they're just taking a guess, Rick said.

I always thought the future would look like the Jetsons, I said.

He turned a page and went humph.

Then we waited more in the waiting room.

Do you think we're getting filmed right now? I asked Rick.

No, they'll tell us when that happens.

Okay good, I said, because I didn't feel like I was from the future yet. Actually I was too bored to feel anything. Plus I guess I was mad we had rode our bikes all day and spent our emergency fund on our party.

I think this is shit work, I told Rick an hour later. I'd rather carry ice blocks.

Then Rick told me to shut up so I kept talking about nothing really just to prove he wasn't the boss.

I felt better when it was time for lunch and we went outside to these big trucks that opened up and had kitchens inside. Us and the other extra people had to line up and wait which was okay because sometimes me and Rick waited for sandwiches at the Gospel Mission so I'm used to it. Rick said all the real actors had food brought to them in their trailers. I told him it was sad they had to live in trailers.

I asked the guy in the truck who had a beard and that knotted rope kind of hair to give me as much food as he could because I was starving. He laughed and piled my plate with all different colors of food. Can you believe this? I said to Rick when we sat down, but he was watching the star actor who was sitting with a pretty lady and an important-looking fat guy who had an old-fashioned hat on his head. Even with my disabled brain and my dead taste buds, I could tell this food had never even seen a can. There was lots of fish and different salads, which I don't like much but ate anyway because I didn't want to get fired. I went back up twice and ate so much my rag and fur future costume got tight and started to rip a little which was okay because you couldn't tell because it was already ripped.

After lunch, we went back and waited in the room for a long

time. Then they said they were wrapping something up and I thought maybe we'd get a present but they just told us to come back tomorrow.

On the way home I asked Rick if he wanted to get some beers to celebrate.

Rick said this wasn't the kind of job where you get paid at the end of the day, we had to wait for our cheques.

How long will that take? I said. I was worried more about having money to eat than I was about drinking any beers.

Dunno, Rick said, could be a while.

Then I realized my disability worker would find out I wasn't disabled when I cashed my cheque.

Don't worry, Rick said, I gave them a fake name instead of your real one and we just sign it over to me and I'll cash it for you. Until then, we're gonna have to live off the lunch truck.

That's all right with me, I said.

We went back every day for a week. Then another week. Rick said we shouldn't ask about our cheques because they'd think we were desperate. I said, Aren't we? and he said, Not yet we aren't.

Our job was to wait in the room for them to call us. We got more used to our future costumes and didn't even bother wearing our nice clothes anymore because nobody really cared, we were all the same anyway once we got dressed up. And some of the other extra people had worse costumes than us like heavy fur robes, fake beards, hats made out of scratchy sticks. It made us feel grateful for ours. I was eating so much at lunch mine barely fit me anymore and I was scared to ask for a bigger one even though they had hundreds more in the other room.

Those nights in our basement Rick didn't talk, which was weird because before he was always putting different complicated plans together like a football coach. He didn't even want to play cards, and usually he hated it when he didn't have any beers to drink but now he didn't seem to care. He did lots of push-ups and went to bed early.

Then one day right after lunch the important fat guy with the hat who I found out was the Assisting Director came into our waiting room and told us finally that they needed us. This was how the movie people talked, they always said they *needed* something when, from as far as I could tell, they more just wanted it. He said they were going to need to have this big explosion in the middle of a street that they had closed down. Then he said he was going to need some people to lead our charge and he started looking around the room. Rick made himself taller and put on his helmet. You, the Assisting Director said to Rick, and you and you, to some other people. Come with me, he said, and they went to the other side of the room. I was happy he didn't pick me because I was worried about tripping over my rags and ruining the movie, but then I was scared I would do something even more stupid without Rick there to tell me it was stupid.

Then the Halifax guy came to the rest of us and told us our motivator, which is like our reason for living. He said we were these hungry, starving people who were trying to get into where some space stuff was so we could take over the spaceships and get back to our planet where there was lots of food and it was also the place where our families lived. It made no sense to me but I looked over at Rick and now that he was one of the leaders he was taking it really serious. I need you to think starving, Halifax guy said to my group and I saw a lady suck in her cheeks. I'd been hungry lots of times in the past, like the time when Rick lost all our money on the way home from the bar or when we had to send money to Rick's dying sister in Halifax, or when we had to buy extra things like our bikes, which Rick got off this guy he knew and were really expensive because they are some of the best racing bikes you can buy. So I just tried to focus on those times but it was hard to believe in my motivator and think starving right after three plates from the lunch truck.

After somebody came to make sure our costumes looked good enough, they took us through some hallways then outside to a street that they'd made to look all burned and wrecked like something really, really bad had happened. There were trucks and movie stuff everywhere. I could see five different cameras and there were tons of people standing around like on the edges of a football field.

They had us wait around more. Then the Director started talking into one of those loud-talking horns. Okay everybody we are only going to do this one time, he said. He was sitting up high on a crane. Someone came and told me to stand in a place. There were lots of us and everybody got their own place. I tried to see Rick but I couldn't see him.

Then all of a sudden I heard Action! and we were all running in a big pack and someone was yelling GoGoGoGo. I was trying not to fall down and my heart was beating like one of those loud things that breaks up the pavement and I started to get a cramp from all of the food that was bouncing around in my belly. A woman ahead of me screamed and tripped over her big stick that had a bird skull at the top and I had to jump over her because if I helped her up I thought I would ruin the movie. Then there was this loud boom behind us and I felt heat go on my ears. I turned and saw the whole front of a building go on fire and there was little bits of stufff lying everywhere and all I could think was that I hoped Rick was okay.

It was the farthest I ever ran and I was almost passing out because my cramp hurt so bad when the Director said cut and they brought us back to the waiting room. Then they got us to take off our costumes and said thanks very much for your time and told us they didn't need us anymore. My legs were still shaking while I went looking for Rick. I walked around for an hour until I saw him still wearing his costume talking with the Halifax guy and the fat Assisting Director over by the trailers.

You can't go in there, a guy with a clipboard said.

In where? I said.

Over there, he said.

So I just biked home.

It had been a few days and I was waiting for the sound of the back gate when Baldev came down the stairs followed by the smell of his country's kind of food that Rick hates but as far as I can tell smells really good, like the lunch truck.

This has come for you, he said, holding out a letter with the government's picture on it. I opened it but I didn't understand what it said because my disabled brain makes it so that I can't read.

Is this from girlfriend? Baldev said, making his big boobs. Let me tell you, Baldev loves big boobs. He puts his hands out in front of his chest to show just how big of boobs he means, which is really, really big. Then he looks down at the boobs and squeezes them. He admires them like he would even settle for having big boobs himself if he ever got the chance. This is maybe the one thing him and Rick agree about.

No, I said, but louder so that he could understand. Baldev, can you read this for me?

Baldev dropped his boobs and took the letter. He saw the government picture at the top and said, No, no, this is not near to my business. Then he went back upstairs.

I sat on a chair trying to make myself read. Once I got a letter from them saying they were going to send somebody to check out whether I was still disabled and see if I could work. After Rick read it out loud, he ripped it up and said there was no way in hell me or my brain was ever going to get better and that they were the ones who needed their heads checked. Then he said something like he always says about how mean the whole world is. Then we sat down and drank beers and felt better. But nobody from welfare ever came, which was good because we didn't want them to see the beers or that the basement was a basement. Now I was worried this letter was another one of those and that maybe this time they really were going to come. I stayed up all night listening to the furnace.

Rick didn't come back the next day or the next. I got hungry and couldn't stop my brain from thinking about the food truck. I wondered if it was still there, because if I could dress up in some old rags and furs again and sneak back, just once, I knew I could eat enough to last me at least a week. Or how maybe they moved the trucks to some other movie somewhere else, and I thought about riding my bike all the way up to Broadway to where Rick said the rich people lived, looking for movie stuff like cranes and things blowing up. But I was too tired. I could have got some emergency money from my worker, Linda, but the letter made me afraid they'd found out I was working as an extra person and they would kick me off like Rick or stick me in jail. I didn't even know where the good dumpster with the donuts in it was because I always just followed Rick.

Then early one morning I woke up to a noise I thought was rats. I turned the light on and saw Rick going through his boxes of stuff.

Oh, hi, he said.

Where you been? I said.

He sat in a chair and leaned his head way back like somebody was washing his hair, and it sounded like he had a cold because he was sniffing lots. I saw he was wearing different shoes and a different coat. They looked new.

Then all of a sudden Rick started talking, not excited like he usually did but still staring up at the boards that I guess were actually holding up Baldev's floor, and even with my bad smell I noticed Rick smelled like lots of beers. He said that after they picked him to be a leader of the future, they gave him a laser rifle that he was supposed to fire at the star. What if you hit him? I asked, and he shut his eyes, blew air out his nose, and said they were going to add the laser beam later. Then Rick said when the Director yelled action and he started running, his helmet slipped over his eyes and he accidentally turned and crashed into the big star right before the huge explosion. He said he was in the only camera angle that they really needed so they had no choice, they had to give him a bigger part in the movie so it didn't seem weird that he was there.

Does that mean our cheques will be bigger? I said.

He said he guessed it did.

Then I asked when we'd get them because I was hungry.

Not yet, he said.

Oh, I said.

It's just like stew, he said. You have to wait. You get impatient.

I asked him if he had any money for us to go get burgers or make something on the hotplate.

No, he said, but there was food and beers at the wrap party. He took a half a sandwich out of his pocket and gave it to me. Is that where you got those clothes? Were they presents from the wrap party? I asked. I was eating the sandwich as slow as I could, picking pocket fluff from my mouth. Yeah, he said. Then he got up and said he would go right then and find out where our cheques were.

I asked him if he could read my letter first.

He grabbed it out of my hand and read it really fast.

It's fine, he said, doesn't mean anything.

There's more on the back, I said.

He flipped it and read the back. It's still fine, he said.

Does it mean they know? I said. That I'm not disabled anymore?

No, he said, and started throwing his things into some grocery bags, but none of his important stuff. And you *are* still goddamn disabled, he said. It just means they don't know their ass from a hole in the ground.

Good, I said.

Then he dropped the bags and put his hands on his face.

You don't have to work anymore, it ain't right for you to, he said.

Especially if it's shit work, I said. Like being extra.

He stood there covering his face for a little bit, breathing weird, and I knew he was really angry because when he took his hands away his face was red and there were veins in it like a bunch of blue candy worms. But then he just gave me a long hug that squeezed my breath and left.

The good part about living with someone is you can sit there and look at their stuff and know they have to come back sometime to get it. He'd left the hot plate and his steeled-toe boots. Sure, he'd taken the pictures of the rotten witch, but he'd left most of his clothes and his favorite baseball cap. I checked outside and he'd left his racing bike, which made me feel even better.

After cleaning the place up a bit I sat for a while on my hunk of foam. I already forgave Rick for getting mad at me because I called his new extra job shit work. He liked to get mad sometimes for bad reasons, so I decided I'd just have to not talk about it ever again and it would be okay. Then I folded up the disabled letter as small as it would go and tried to throw it in the garbage but I missed. I was thinking about how, after working as an extra person from the future for so long, it was like I was becoming a professional waiter, and how that now I could wait for pretty well anything as long as I knew it was coming. I thought about how long it would take for my belly to eat the sandwich Rick gave me, and about how long it would be before my disabled brain wouldn't be able to stop me from following the smell of Baldev's wife's food up the stairs and knocking on their door. I didn't know how long that would be.

MIRANDA HILL

PETITIONS TO SAINT CHRONIC

Twenty-four storeys straight down and what else to call it but miracle? Twenty-four storeys and not a scratch on him: that would be a miracle for sure. But twenty-four storeys and massive internal hemorrhage, broken spine, complete loss of consciousness, and drugs to sedate him if he ever does come out of it – that's Gibson.

Carlos tells me not to quibble. Says everyone receives God's gifts – some of us just don't recognize them. But Gibson will believe.

Micheline is planning on making Gibson a better man. She tells us he will look fine in a well-cut suit, silk tie, polished shoes. Micheline calls Gibson "pure potential."

Carlos says that's denying what Gibson is already. "He doesn't need to ascend. The last shall be first. He is the least of us, and he is loved."

The cleaner mopping the floor past our orange vinyl chairs out by the elevator bank, down the hall from the ICU, says,

"Some people shouldn't be allowed to breed. If this guy doesn't die I'll lose my faith in Darwin."

A nurse in green scrubs comes around the corner, down the long hall, and past the sign that says, "ICU. Visitors must be signed in." She nods to another nurse at the reception desk and presses the down button beside the elevator. Her eyes are all apology. "Only next of kin," she says. We've heard that for days, but no family is coming for Gibson. It's just Carlos, Micheline, and me. Twenty-four storeys, and we three strangers are all he's got.

Each of us saw Gibson on the all-day news. The reporter had hair that was blowing in the mild summer breeze. He tried to hold our attention. Even before we turned the sound up, his face said, "The world is full of peril, but I will lead you through in my pressed linen shirt." But the camera wanted to follow Gibson, small like a bug in the corner of the screen. It loved him as we loved him. It was hard to tell what the crowd was chanting, but the volume seemed to rise as Gibson stretched his arms out like a conductor. Then he stepped into the air and fell.

The day that Gibson was brought in, a reporter outside Emergency asked Micheline how long she had known Gibson. "I am not his past," she said. "I am his future." She spelled her name, but the reporter didn't write it down. I asked her to spell it again. "It's French," she said. "One *l*."

By the time Carlos got there, most of Emergency was empty. Just a broken arm and chest pains and a couple of reporters using the pay phones because the nurses wouldn't let them use their cells. But by then the shifts had changed and Micheline and I weren't making any trouble. We could have been waiting there for anyone.

Carlos must have come straight from the garage because he was still in coveralls with a Ford insignia and oil down the front, but he was wearing a thick gold cross and carrying a Bible. He burst through the swinging doors, then stood in the middle of the waiting room as if he had suddenly lost his way.

"Where can I find the man who fell?" he called out, and the nurse closed the little glass partition between her and the rest of us.

"Hey, Father Ford!" said the Floor Guy.

"I am not a priest. I am a supplicant."

"Yeah? Well you're standing in my pile."

Micheline waved her hand in Carlos's direction as if she were wafting away someone else's cigarette smoke. But I lifted up my bag and made a spot for him on the seat beside me.

The doctors give their reports to the media. The media relay them. We arrange our morning meeting place – on the bench outside, where the families of the patients go to smoke – and read the reports. The photographs show Gibson to be dark haired with skin like wax paper over veins of seaweed sprawl. We hold the papers on our knees as we drink coffee that I have brought from the all-night diner one block away. It is too early for the cafeteria to be open.

We turn the pages back. Carlos says Gibson is pale so that the light can shine through him. Micheline says he needs a little more sun. She will take him to Florida, she says, when he is well enough to stand the drive. To me, he looks as vulnerable as those girls in high school whose hips jutted up against the pocket rivets of their jeans. The ones everyone always tiptoed around: a fracture waiting to happen. The world pressed in closer on those among us who were cushioned by flesh, as if that offered sufficient protection. Despite the skin and the veins, Gibson has hands that look big and capable. They look like hands that could have hung on. But there are things you can't know from looking.

The first time my husband hit me, we were in the bathroom, so it was hard to tell whether the darker bruise was from Cy's hand or from the edge of the sink I hit going down. I felt across the floor to see if I would find blood, but the tiles were dry. When I pulled myself up, I held onto the vanity and stood in front of the mirror as long as I could. The red was spreading under my skin, my cheek and my forehead swelling. It looked like it should hurt. I couldn't even remember Cy's fist on me. It was as if something had pushed its way out from the inside like a latent cancer. "This is how I look as a beaten woman," I said. I tried it on like a uniform, and felt it settle on me like something I was always meant to wear.

Micheline says it must have been a woman that crushed Gibson's spirit. Carlos says, "Why does everyone always think that only women hold such power? There are other things that can destroy a man."

Carlos is worried about what will happen if he is at work when Gibson comes to, when they finally allow him a visitor. "Will you tell him God is love?" he asks me. "Will you tell him for me?"

Micheline says that when he wakes up we will give him the choice of the two of us, confident that he will select her. I could play along, tell her I want a man who is already dismantled, so I don't have to do the job myself or stand by and watch it happen. That I plan to buy us matching T-shirts that will announce our condition: Damaged. That when we walk, people will hear what is left of us rattle.

But to each of them I let my smile answer for me. Let them believe what they will. I am not interested in his recovery. You can sew a body up again, but that doesn't make it whole.

Outside Ultrasound no one asks any questions and they have a good TV. While we wait for the press conference to begin, Micheline and I flip through celebrity magazines and she passes on old gossip about washed-up stars. Micheline tells me she has been a child actress, a cartoon voice, a hit songwriter. She makes enough from her songs to never work again, except for licensing the rights to ad agencies for commercials. She tells me I would know these songs if she hummed them, but she doesn't take requests. Now she is more of a scout, she says.

"Take Gibson," she says. But really, why would you? Nobody would imagine that he could be turned around and become the kind of guy who would buy tickets to Cirque du Soleil, book a holiday on a romantic island, wear a Kiss the Cook apron when he barbecues steak with the neighbours. Nobody except Micheline.

Micheline opens her purse and hands me one of her success stories: a photo of a man with hair greying at the temples. Beside him is a woman with streaked blonde hair pulled into a ponytail, holding a fat-faced baby. An old lover, made into a new man, then released: Micheline's gift to the world. "From

AA to Executive, Silicon Valley," she says. Micheline is the thirteenth step.

Eight hours, twelve hours, split shifts – all around us, the nurses and doctors move through their rotations. For a week now, we three have also split our vigil into days and nights of waiting. We arrange our meeting places, watch for security, adhere to our schedule. Micheline arrives at six a.m., asking if there are any developments. Just before she comes, I go get the morning papers and new coffee for our breakfast overlap. Then Carlos goes to work, returning to relieve Micheline at eight p.m. We are all together for an hour or so and then Micheline leaves. I pretend to Micheline that I go when she does, but I return with Raisinettes and pretzels from the machine to the place that Carlos and I have decided to wait through the night.

They each think that I sleep when they sleep, I watch when they watch. If they notice that I only wear two different shirts and two pairs of pants, if they see that I don't change this old sweater, they never say a thing.

In the back of the hospital chapel, Carlos tells me he wants to talk about where we were when we saw him. Carlos says he was standing over the engine of a car that wouldn't start. It was his first day on a real job, he tells me, a legal one, the first he'd had in this country, and now the car refused to come to life. He tried all his usual cures: something with wires, with belts. "Just trust me, I can get a car going. It's my talent. But this one was dead," he says. "Think of the heat that day. Think of no air conditioning." As he bent over the engine, the crucifix around his neck dangled in front of his eyes, blocking his view. He says he threw it back over his shoulder, so it wouldn't distract him from the job.

While the other guys in the bay turned up the sound on the twenty-four-hour news and gathered under the TV set, Carlos kept working. The sweat was pouring into his eyes. This is a test, he was thinking. He breathed in the smell of old engine. Then the guys started hollering: The bastard's going to jump! When Gibson hit the ground, the car started. Carlos watched the jump in repeat, impact after impact.

"So, where were you?" Carlos asks. But my eyes are closing. Carlos balls up his jacket and makes a nest of it in the corner of the pew and I lay my head against the old tweed. Beside me, Carlos smells like roses. When his fingers press the rosary beads the skin is pink and clean, but at the end of every nail, a rim of grease.

When I was in grade nine I had a friend called Lesley-Anne whose parents were breaking up. Lesley-Anne sat beside me in science class, in those big double desks with the sinks in the middle. The kids on Lesley-Anne's street said there had been screaming and crying, there had been accusations of other lovers, there were battles over the children. But Lesley-Anne only mentioned it once. "Their marriage exploded," she said. She didn't look at me, just doodled in the margins of the science textbook that we shared. That night, I looked at the ink ellipses spinning out like some ever-changing orbit beside a diagram of the Big Bang, electric blue and orange on a black background. From then on I believed that that was how marriages ended, in a storm of meteors, bright and loud enough the neighbours were bound to hear.

So it was never the heat and the bursting that amazed me with Cy, it was the numbness that followed. The leeside of the hitting was like the dark side of the moon.

It was quiet for days, weeks, months. The bigger the explosion, the more time it took to repair, but it happened all the same. Fractures, dislocations, bruises – the torn pieces of me just fused together again like a trap door closing over an empty hole. Sometimes Cy would stay home and tend to me, press a washcloth up against the stitches. Shh, shh, he'd say, and I'd barely even feel them. But other times, the times he would go away, I could feel the longing for him sharper than any of the splits in my skin. I will leave when it gets harder to stay than to go, I told myself. I was waiting for something worse – an injury so severe that it would break us forever, make it impossible to recover. But something in me refused to stay broken. I couldn't escape my ability to heal.

On the tenth day after Gibson's fall, the doctors give a press conference and the elevators to Intensive Care fill up with reporters on their way to the media room. I bring up our takeout lunches the back way – through Emergency to Physio, where they have a television we have not watched before.

A dozen frustrated patients try to catch the nurse's attention, hoping to be called. She keeps her eyes on the desk, except when she lifts them to stare at me.

On the television, a middle-aged man and woman are mooning at each other across a breakfast table while three teenagers show increasingly obvious signs of revolt, from rolling their eyes to packing cake and beer in their lunch bags. The couple continues to smile and blush, oblivious. The voice on the television lists side effects and encourages us to talk to our doctor.

"One of mine," says Micheline.

The commercial finishes before I realize that she means the song, a tune about perpetual sunshine, its words just beyond familiar.

"It was playing the afternoon I saw Gibson," Micheline says. She was waiting in a hotel bar for her lunch date – another former lover. Once an army private. "Gifted, but directionless."

And now?

"Harvard. Magna cum laude. He was in town for a conference."

At the hotel, she says, the TV over the bar showed the midday news with the volume off, while a medley of old hits played over the sound system. Just as Micheline heard her young voice played back to her, there was Gibson, standing on the window ledge while Micheline sang about beaches forever. The song played right through Gibson's fall. But Micheline asked the bartender to turn up the sound on the TV. When the reporter said Gibson was alive, Micheline threw a twenty on the counter, left a message for her Harvard man, and took a cab to the hospital downtown.

The nurse at the desk is staring at me. "You look familiar," she says.

"I was here yesterday," I tell her.

Beside me, Micheline's magazine flutters shut. "This isn't a good place," she says. "Let's go to Same Day Surgery."

She doesn't notice how the nurse watches me as I lift my purse and walk to the elevator.

—

The media reported the profound effect of Gibson's fall on the people who were there to witness it. A woman cried and fainted. People vomited. Others rushed in before emergency crews arrived to see if they could help. But where are they now, asks Carlos, if he spoke to them so directly? "The three of us received his call at a distance, and we came. That is what it means to believe," he says.

Carlos tells me about Saint Clare of Assisi, the patron saint of television, a noblewoman who heard Francis of Assisi speak and founded the order of Poor Clares, women who lived an ascetic existence, surviving on alms. When she was old and too ill to go to mass, the mass would appear on the wall of her little cell. When he prays for Gibson, Carlos prays to Saint Clare, he prays to Saint Jude for desperate causes, he prays to the Virgin, too.

Micheline is tired of his sermons. She shoves her chair back from the cafeteria table and our cups tremble, coffee spilling over the sides. We watch her push through the doors and out to the hall.

I ask Carlos: who is the saint for causes almost lost, for causes of the ultimate draw, the endless overtimes, who is the patron saint of those who can't lose themselves no matter how hard they try?

"Blessed are the pure of heart, for they shall see God," Carlos says.

The Floor Guy mops silently around our feet, then pushes his cart into the kitchen. His voice echoes off the stainless steel as the door swings closed: "Blessed are the self-destructive, for they shall save the rest of us the trouble."

—

Micheline meets us in the lobby with a pie she has made herself. "Practice, for Gibson," she says. The Floor Guy sneers as he wrings out his mop. "He'll never give up the liquid lunch," he says.

"Self-improvement only requires inner movement," she says. Then she cuts him the first slice. "You should try it."

Micheline says there are skills every woman should master. She says she can tell I am the kind of woman who knows this. She asks me to think of my greatest talent. I laugh. She doesn't understand that this is my answer. An easy laugh reveals my one true talent: I have the gift of acquiescence.

I am better versed in the things that a woman should not do. Keep your chin up and your skirt down. I have remembered the saying, but confused the order. Of all the instructions I have ever been given, it seems I have done the opposite of everything but floss. When the dentist on call saw my teeth in the little dish, he complimented my hygiene. "If it were up to you, these would have been biting into apples until you were one hundred." As if I had nothing to do with it. As if the place I'd put myself in had nothing to do with where I was now. As if this weren't just another of my animal defenses I'd surrendered.

The pie is lemon and the pastry flakes away in sheets. Micheline accepts our compliments and tells us she is self-taught. Carlos says the crust reminds him of the layers of stone in the quarry in the town he grew up in. "Rock Bottom?" asks the Floor Guy, but he holds his plate out for more.

After two weeks, the press conferences are less frequent. The statements shorter. I have stopped trying to identify the specialists. But Micheline watches, trying to read between the lines, to determine a more accurate prognosis.

Each day over the intercom there are calls for doctors to dash to patients in various states of trauma. We imagine every call to be for Gibson. If we are near the patient elevators, we wait for the doors to open, in case we can get a glimpse of him while they rush him to another effort to repair one more tear in his river of ruptured functions.

When a patient goes by on a dais of hospital linen, barricaded by nurses that obscure his face, our voices lower; it might be him.

"If he lives, I will tell him we know it was only a cry for help," says Carlos, collapsing his rosary beads in his hand.

"Just wait till he finds out who answered," says the Floor Guy, and he mops under the television in a place that already looks clean.

Micheline says Gibson has been moved to a step-down unit.

"What does that mean?" I ask. "Does that mean he's getting better?"

"It means less security," she says. "Soon they'll have to let us in."

She stakes out a place on the new floor, flipping through the same old issues of the magazines that are stacked in every waiting room.

I walk Carlos to the bus stop and then I go back to the disabled bathroom on the first floor and scrub at my extra pair of underwear with an old toothbrush I have dipped into the Floor Guy's bleach. The smell is all the hospital's comfort, its promise of someone else in charge – so much control, so little attention. It makes me sleepy. These are the things that keep me here: Gibson, and, when I am away from him, bleach.

I sit on the low toilet seat and lean my head against the wall to keep me from tumbling off while my eyes are closed.

The last time I was discharged from the hospital, I bleached the sheets three times to get the stain out, running them through cold water in the basement of my building, sitting guard at the washer's glass window. When they came white again, I went to stretch them out over the bed and saw that the blood had seeped deep into the mattress. Before Gibson, at night, I would lie over the stain as if it were an inland sea, trying to draw the baby back up into me like water into a cloud.

The nurse in Emergency told me, "If you do not press charges, this will happen again and again."

It was when I lost the baby that I knew I would always take him back. But this time it was Cy who stayed away. I spoke to him in our silent apartment. I spoke to him as if he were there, "Come home, Cy. I promise I'll take you back. I will heal and take you back, forever."

And I would have, before Gibson.

I do not know how long I have been asleep in the bathroom, but when I come back to the new waiting room, Micheline is not in her chair. I sit for a minute, resting a coffee on each knee, waiting. Wondering where she might have gone. Nearby, there is a bathroom for the disabled, but the door is open and no one is inside. I want to ask where the other bathroom is, but there is no nurse at the station. I go down and around the hall. I find the bathroom, but Micheline is not in it.

The hall is quiet. A doctor passes, but doesn't ask my business. I stand in the new silence and listen. I hear only my own persistent breathing, my own belligerent heart. And an occasional banging.

There is a "Wet Floor" sign around the corner. The Floor Guy moves the mop back and forth, from one wall to the other, raising a damp shine between us. It is a long time before he looks up. Surprised, his face is soft as a chamois.

"Hello. Come to roll away the stone?"

"What happened to Micheline?"

"Packed up and went, I imagine. She must be disappointed. Hardly a return on her investment." A woman in a silk cardigan walks down the hall, carrying flowers, then turns the corner.

"I don't know what you mean," I say.

The Floor Guy pulls the bucket toward him and leans on the handle of his mop, studying my face. He bends, picks up the sign, and jerks his head so that I will follow. We turn the way the woman went, and then turn again, passing closed doors with little windows at the top that look into rooms. He stops and pushes one open, unfolding the Wet Floor sign in front of it. He nudges me forward at the shoulder.

Pink curtains are closed around a bed in the middle of the room. I step forward and push my arms through the opening in the fabric, pulling back as if I am diving into deep water.

The sheet is over Gibson's body, covering even his face. Wires and tubes run out from under the sheet, but the machines they connect him to are quiet, their screens dark, the cords disconnected. At a spot halfway up the bed, I lift the sheet to look for something recognizable. His hand is mostly bandaged, the sides of his fingers are purple.

I think of what it was Carlos wanted to say to him, of the songs that Micheline planned to sing in her beckoning voice.

But it's me who is speaking, telling Gibson our story – his and mine – taking it back to the beginning, to the moment I saw him on television, saw him fall. But wait, that doesn't give us enough time. I stretch it out. I tell him about what came before. The cat food commercial, essential nutrients for the senior feline. And then the one for paint that goes straight on over rust, you don't even have to scrub. No. More. Back before that, to the phone ringing, to the voice I thought I'd always be waiting for, back to Cy saying, "Forgive me darling, forgive me. I'm coming home."

My hand curls around Gibson's fingers. For a miracle, he is very cold and still. I warm my palm with my breath and lift his hand to my chest. His arm is heavy and splinted. I tell Gibson that after he fell the TV showed the crowd closing in and the paramedics arriving and the way the reporter announced he was alive by saying: "It's a miracle. What else could you call it?"

I tell Gibson how I packed my bag and called a cab. How I left the TV on in the apartment so that Cy could fill those empty rooms and make them his own. I knew that when Cy got there, the news would probably have changed to arson or stabbings or blowout sales, but by then I would be free.

I shift my hip onto the bed and wedge myself in beside Gibson, next to the metal bed rail, lay my head on the edge of the pillow, and whisper it all again: the phone call, the commercial, Gibson falling, packing my suitcase, calling the cab. But my eyes are closing, and the sequence seems confusing. Is it the cat food commercial and then the one for paint? I am so very tired. The phone rings. I see Gibson. I pack. I see Gibson and I am packing. But now I am packing through the cat food, and the rust remover. I am packing through Gibson's fall and even packing through Cy's phone call. And I can see that I am already leaving. I am leaving. I am leaving before I see Gibson and even before the phone rings, so that when Gibson falls I stretch my arms wide too – to catch him, or hold him, or look with him all the way down.

ROSS KLATTE

FIRST-CALF HEIFER

Carl opened his eyes. It was late. It was too light outside his window.

He raised the window, put his head near the screen, and listened. Chilled October air sifted in, and he saw frost on the roof of the pump house. A flock of sparrows broke noisily out of a tree and went bounding away in the sky.

He strained to listen. When he was sure he couldn't hear the purr of the vacuum motor in the barn, he relaxed a little. He jumped out of bed and dressed in his cold room.

Downstairs the kitchen clock said six-thirty. His father would have called him at six. Could it be he hadn't called him this morning? No. *I'm gonna get it*, Carl thought.

The barn was empty. The little piles of ground corn and oats were before each stanchion. His father himself must be getting the cows.

Damn it, Carl thought. He was going to get it.

In the milkhouse, next to the barn, he found the milking machines, the strainer, and the milk cans needed rinsing and setting up. He went to work at this, feeling better. He was rinsing the six ten-gallon cans with scalding water and disinfectant when he heard the familiar click of split hooves and blowing of nostrils in the barnyard. The cows were home.

He stepped into the barn and closed both halves of the Dutch door. Then he opened the door to the barnyard and the cows came pushing and heaving in, going hungrily to their own stanchions. Carl walked up and down the manger, closing the stanchions, waiting for his father to appear – waiting to receive his anger. The last cow entered the barn, followed by his father, who closed the door behind her. He looked sternly at Carl, then strode past him into the silo room, and came out with a pail of extra feed for the best cows. Carl got the machines from the milkhouse. He scraped the floor clean where the cows had dirtied it.

"Well, for once you did somethin' right, I must say," his father began. "You did me a favour by laying in bed this morning."

Carl didn't say anything.

"Yup, it's just a good goddamn thing it was me got the cows this morning and not you."

His father was no taller than Carl now, but his bulk, his anger at Carl that often exploded into belittling verbal abuse, was still threatening. Carl wasn't that afraid of his father anymore, but he knew better than to stand up to him; someday, maybe, but not yet.

"You know that heifer with the black over one eye?"

"She had her calf," Carl said, knowing that was it.

"That's right." His father wiped his nose with the back of his hand. Carl noticed the hand was dirty, streaked a kind of rusty brown. "She was tryin' to have it when I found her."

"I thought she wasn't due yet."

"Yeah, well so did I. I shoulda known better. I shoulda kept her in the barn. You gotta watch these first-calf heifers. They get bred out in the pasture and then you gotta punch 'em and try to guess when they're comin' in. Yeah, it's just a damn good thing it was *me* that found her," his father said. "You wouldn't a known what to do."

"I would've known enough to get you," Carl said.

"Yeah, well, what if I wasn't around to get? You ever think of that?"

"I've thought about it," said Carl.

"It was too big," his father said. "I had ta pull for all I was worth to get it outa her. I think I hurt her a little."

"The calf dead?"

"Yeah, *long* dead."

"The heifer all right?"

"I dunno. She might be ruined."

His father turned away from Carl and hit the switch that started the vacuum motor. Then he picked up a milker. He drew the washrag out of the pail of warm, disinfected water and gently, soothingly washed the teats of the first cow in line. He pitched the rag back into the pail, splashing Carl with the water. Then his father swung the strap around the cow, slung the milker under her, and lifted each teat cup into place. Then he washed the next cow in line and grabbed the other milker.

"Look, tonight you go out there and find her," he told Carl. "If she's still down, get'er up. Bring her in, yuh understand? But take her easy, real easy. She's had a tough time, that little heifer."

"Where is she?"

"Over by the line fence, in the swamp pasture." His father looked at Carl with his heavy face. "Goddamn it, you know how much a cow and calf are worth?"

"No."

"You wouldn't." his father said. "Well, don't just stand there with yur finger up yur ass. You goin' to school?"

"Yeah."

"Then *go*, goddammit," his father told him.

His mother looked up when Carl opened the door to the kitchen. She was helping his baby brother, little Harold, button his jacket.

"Hurry up, you'll miss your bus," she said. Her patient, tired face looked up at him.

His kid brother, Billy, came clumping down the stairs, and then his younger sister, Janey, came regally down and sat at the kitchen table.

"Janey, hurry up and eat," their mother said.

"I'm hurrying, Ma," Janey said, but she took her time.

His mother would drive Janey and Carl's brothers to the Catholic grade school in New Dresden. Carl, just fourteen, had started the public high school in Sioux Lake.

He just had time to wash, change out of his barn clothes, dip some toast in coffee, then run out to the head of their long driveway to catch the bus.

On the school bus he felt better. On the bus, and in school, he was away from the farm; away from the work. He was away from his father.

He had hated parochial school. His sister Janey was hating

it now. But he liked the public high school. He was sort of coasting along this first year there on what he had learned from the nuns. He was unlearning some things too, such as not bothering to stand up when the teacher called you. Some of the girls had tittered when he first did that. Now he slouched in his seat and was a little bit of a smart aleck. It was what he had learned from the other students. He liked high school, too, because of the girls. They were tougher, more exciting, than the girls at sister school. And they dressed in exciting ways – in tight jeans, for instance, that hugged their cute little behinds. He was learning a lot about girls in the boys' locker room, where he got into shorts and a jock-strap for gym class in the morning and into sweat clothes for wrestling practice in the afternoon. Like most farm boys, he was out for wrestling, and like all of them, he had been surprised at his own strength when he went up against a town kid, some kid from one of the swell houses around the lake, whose father worked in a suit in the city and who would have been better at something like basketball – "pussy" ball – where you could be flashy and didn't need any strength. Some of the farm boys went out for football, too, but Carl was too light for that. He was out for one of the lighter weights in wrestling.

There were girls from those swell houses around the lake whom Carl wanted to "breed." That's how farm boys put it. There was one girl he wanted to hump like a bull if he ever got the chance. He'd know what to do. He'd seen some pictures in a guy's locker, one of which showed a woman on her back with her legs spread and a man about to shove it to her. Another was a close-up, not of a woman exactly, but of what a woman had between her legs.

"Ever seen *that*, you farmers?" the guy said, looking directly at Carl, "except on a cow?"

Carl stepped off the bus that afternoon, weary from wrestling practice. His neck was stiff and his shoulders ached from a practice match he'd had with another farm kid. It was never an easy match with another farm kid. The kid had almost pinned him, but then Carl had won on points.

He walked down the long driveway to the house. In the late afternoon the sun was weak and far down in the sky, but there was light and quiet in the air. He felt the quiet, the pause, in the air. He felt apart, suspended, not in school or on the farm, but in between somewhere, somewhere suspended, in a kind of pause. It was always pleasant in this quiet pause at the end of day.

In the house his mother and Janey were making supper. Billy and Harold were in the living room listening to the radio serials he wished he could still listen to. They had their little chores – picking the eggs, feeding the chickens – but it was Carl now who did a man's work for his father.

"Dad said you might have to start the milking," his mother told him.

"Yeah, he out plowing?" Carl said. He began to fill up on cookies and milk.

"Yes, and he said he'll keep at it till after dark."

"Okay."

"You know about that heifer you're supposed to look for?"

"Oh, yeah, that's right," Carl said, remembering.

"Better get going then."

"I'm going, I'm going," Carl told his mother.

He changed into his old jeans and work shoes. Then he went out to the porch, where his and his father's barn clothes were hung out to air, and got into his overalls. He buckled on his overshoes, then put on his hat and jacket.

"You going to eat before you start the milking?" his mother asked. She had opened the kitchen door.

"I better not," Carl said. "He'll be mad if I haven't started."

In the barn he laid out feed before the stanchions. The gutters needed shoveling out, but he would do that later. His first job was to get the cows. He went out the barnyard door, closed it, and walked down the cowpath to the swamp pasture.

The sun was just setting. It was chilly already. Carl walked down into a layer of frigid air as he descended into the swamp. This time of year the swamp was mostly dry, with only pockets of wet in places. The tall slough grass was getting brown and bent over from frost. There was frost nearly every night now. In spring the swamp formed a shallow lake, where migrating ducks landed, and in summer there were hidden pools under the clumps of willow, where ducks nested. It wasn't till fall that the swamp could be used as pasture.

Only last week it had been Indian summer. There'd been days so warm, so lovely, so full of leaves in the air and leaves underfoot that Carl had wanted to stretch out in all that softness, the softness in the air and on the ground. But it was ended now. It was starting to turn cold and grey, the grey sky seeming to touch the ground. It was the grey season.

It was the season – and high school this year wasn't making any difference – when Carl felt most hopeless. He was filled with the deep hopelessness of life, of his life on the farm, the only life he had known and might ever know. He saw his life as it was – without change. The only change was in the seasons.

It was always better when it snowed finally and winter had come. Then the country was like a picture in black and white: the white fields and the stands of black, leafless trees. It was like a block print he'd seen once in a book.

He found the herd in the middle of the swamp, still grazing in the waist-high grass. The cold air was settling in the swamp and a faint mist was rising. There would be a hard frost tonight. In the morning the swamp would be white with frost, white as if with snow.

"Come boss, come baaass," Carl called.

The cows threw up their heads to look at him. A few started for home. The rest began to pull hastily at the long grass, their eyes rolling back to watch him. It was a little game they played. It was a kind of teasing.

"Go on, *go home*," Carl said. A cow would start away, then stop to pull furtively at the grass. "Hey! Go home!" Carl said, running at them.

At last he had them bunched up and moving. A few held back, but he drove them into an udder-swaying run and they joined the herd. With the herd in a line on the path to the barn, he gave a count: twenty-six, barring the youngstock. The first-calf heifer was missing.

He began to push through the grass toward the line fence, where his father had left her that morning. She was still there. Her calf, the calf his father had pulled out of her, lay stiff, its eyes glazed, beside her, and she herself was on her side, her legs stiffly out, her tongue out, her eyes rolling back into her head. She was having another calf.

He looked toward the herd, strung out and plodding toward the barnyard. It was dark enough now he could just see them. He listened, and heard the tractor. His father was still plowing, away off in the field on the other side of the woods that bordered the swamp. He would keep working, by the lights on the tractor, until he'd finished the field.

Why wasn't he here? It was like his father wasn't here on purpose, like he was teaching Carl a lesson.

He looked at the heifer – her eyes rolled back – and knew he would have to help her. He would have to try, anyhow.

The heifer's vagina was terribly dilated, split, and bleeding. The placenta was like a bubble coming out of her, and she had stopped pushing. The bubble was stuck. Inside the bubble, through the membrane of the placenta, Carl could see the nose and front hooves of the calf. "Well, at least you're not backaswards," he told it.

He poked his finger into the membrane. He broke through and the fluid came pouring out. He took grass and wiped the slime from the calf's nostrils, so it could breathe. Then he knew it was dead.

"All right," he told the heifer. "We still got to get it out."

He was shaking now, not only from the cold, as he took hold of the calf's legs, braced his own against the heifer's backside, and pulled. The heifer bellowed.

"I know, I know it hurts," he told her.

He pulled more grass and wiped the slime from the calf's legs. He took off his jacket and felt the cold and took hold of the calf's legs again. He pulled and pulled, wanting the heifer to push. The heifer let out another bellow, and Carl said, "I know it hurts, but you gotta push, girl. C'mon now. *Push.*"

He pulled. He pulled and pulled, and the calf gave just a little. He caught his breath, took another hold, and pulled, felt the heifer push, and they pulled and pushed together until Carl felt something give inside the calf and thought it was coming, then realized he'd only dislocated the shoulder. But it was dead anyway and so he pulled again and pulled with the heifer not helping anymore, pulled until he thought his heart would burst. He had to stop.

"It's no use," he told himself. A wave of his old hopelessness washed over him. He wanted to cry.

He heard his father's tractor in the distance. "God damn you!" he called to him. "Why aren't you here?"

It was dark now. It was an eerie, whitish darkness, from the cold mist rising out of the swamp. He stood up to catch his breath. The air was so cold it hurt to take it in. He was sweating and cold at the same time. He looked across to the lighted house, like light far away in space. Below, where the barn was, it was dark. He wished he saw a light in the barn. That would mean his father was home finally and wondering where Carl was and why he hadn't started the milking.

He knew what he would have to do now. He'd seen his father do it, and had thought he could never do it himself.

He stripped to his undershirt and the air was like cold metal on his bare arms. He got down on his knees behind the heifer, pulled her tail aside, and forced his right hand and then the length of his arm up into her, into that poor, distended, ripped opening, taut as stretched leather, until he broke through to the hot womb behind the calf. He was in up to his armpit. The heifer bellowed and kicked at Carl.

"Sooo, boss," he told her soothingly. "I'm trying to help!"

She bucked and bellowed as he felt around inside her, felt the calf's hind leg, the one bent and caught inside her. He worked at it, twisted and pushed, until it straightened suddenly, and just then the heifer jerked and emptied her bowels over Carl. He felt it hot and heavy on his shoulder and down his back.

He eased his arm out and stood up and shook himself. Most of the shit fell away. He pulled grass and wiped his arm and shoulder and what he could reach of his back. His undershirt was wet and cold against his skin. He took it off and used it to wipe the calf's forelegs again. *It's no use,* he thought, but he knelt again and grabbed the calf's forelegs and pulled. He pulled and pulled, but it wouldn't come. Then he sat down, not caring anymore, braced his feet against the heifer's backside, pulled, and the calf came slithering out, *slop*, like an enormous discharge of waste. It was all waste.

He fell back on the grass. Presently he got up and went around to the heifer. He could just make out her head in the darkness. He felt for her eyes. They didn't blink when he touched them.

"Aw," Carl said to the darkness. He was so tired, he felt sick.

He lay on the grass, listening to himself breathing. The dark forms of the heifer and her calves were quiet. Then he saw a light and heard something coming toward him through the grass. "Carl?" his father called.

"Here!"

His father came up with a flashlight and stooped to examine the heifer. Then he went to the calf. Then he moved toward Carl. The light was blinding and his father was a dark shape behind it.

"She's still warm," he said.

"Yeah, she just died," Carl said.

"Twins!" his father said. "Who woulda guessed it?"

"I should've gone and got you, Dad."

"Naw, I don't think that would've mattered. You weren't late getting the cows, though, were you?"

Carl felt a rush of the old anger, the old helpless rage before his father's questioning of his ability. There was nothing he could say.

"Anyway, it was my fault," his father said. "I shoulda checked on her today. I mighta saved her."

Carl began to feel in the grass for his shirt. He found it, it was wet and cold, but he put it on.

"Well, it's been quite a day," his father said now. "We lost a cow and two calves today."

Carl felt the weight of that loss and wanted to feel it. He wanted to bear some of it for his father.

"Aw, well. Live and learn," his father said, which was something he often said.

They started across the swamp toward the farm buildings. There were lights in the barn now. His father must have turned them on and let the cows in the barn before he came looking for him.

He stopped.

"What's wrong?" his father asked.

"My jacket. I left it back there."

"Here, take the light," said his father. But Carl was already running back through the high grass in the darkness. He stumbled over the bodies of the heifer and her calves. He felt around for his jacket, found it, and put it on. He bent and touched the heifer. She was cold already, damp with the dew that was turning to frost in the darkness.

Then he was running back to where his father stood waiting for him. Together they walked to the barn to start the evening chores.

JESSICA WESTHEAD

WHAT I WOULD SAY

I haven't been to a party before where they served pie, have you? But I guess that's a silly question because of course you'd know the hosts, so you've probably – Anyway, it's very good pie. It takes creative people to come up with a snack idea like that.

I said to Appollonia – that's who I came with – "Would you have thought of giving out pie?" And she said, "Nope." But of course Appollonia is not creative like you and me. Which she wouldn't mind me saying, by the way. We all have our strengths and weaknesses.

Now me, I've got my chapbook. But put an equation in front of me and do you think I'd know how to solve it? Give me a break! I am a words person whereas Appollonia is a numbers person, which is a skill so many of us writers and publishers haven't mastered. On the other hand, Appollonia is not a big reader. She has a subscription to *Chatelaine*, if that tells you anything. She also watches a lot of television. Let's just say she has her shows.

By saying that, I am not saying Appollonia is a bad person. Far from it. She is kind, and holds a special place in her heart for society's cast-offs. There are just some things she doesn't understand – will never understand – because she is Appollonia, and she is a different person from you and me. A good person, certainly. But a different person. Let's just say she is mainstream, and leave it at that. I mean, she's one of my good friends, and I know her, and she would not think the label "mainstream" was a negative thing.

Do you remember earlier, when "Panama" came on? She said to me, "Who sings this, again?" And I said, "It doesn't matter, Appollonia – they're playing it ironically." But she started bopping her head to it anyway. That's just the way she is. And she says the funniest things! What was it she said the other day – she's no poet but she just comes out with the greatest turns of phrase. Oh, I remember. She was talking about her work – she works in an office, as in permanently – and she was explaining how she'd stood up to her boss about switching the complimentary coffee milk from two per cent to one per cent. Now, I'm sorry, but if you're putting it in your coffee, you cannot tell the difference between one per cent and two per cent, it's impossible. If you're drinking the milk on its own, then maybe. But otherwise not in a million years. And these people were up in arms about it! So they had a meeting and Appollonia called for a vote for two per cent, which she knew was the consensus, but none of her co-workers backed her up, so it was just her against the boss. And do you know what she said to me at the end of her anecdote? She said, "They hung me out to frigging hang myself." Isn't that wonderful?

I asked her once for permission to write a poem about her work life. Because it is so unpoetic, there's actually an irony at work there – ha! – that's worth writing about. And Appollonia said to me, "Sure, what the hell. Immortalize me." Isn't that perfect? The things she comes out with.

Between you and me? Appollonia has lived a terrible life.

Her parents were gypsies, which is bad enough, but while at least most gypsies are known for their flair for performance, Appollonia's gypsy parents were bookkeepers. And I'm not talking librarians, which would've been something, right? So, you know, they moved around a lot. Up until she started kindergarten, Appollonia was uprooted I can't even tell you how many times. Over and over again, suffice it to say.

But she is not a complainer. Never has been. I met her in grade one, we were in the same class, and the other kids would throw blocks at her and she wouldn't say boo. That's what first intrigued me about her, actually. She also has that voice – you must know her voice, where it always sounds like she's about to burst into tears, like "Huhhh, huhhh, huhhhn," all the time, but she's not, it's just the way she sounds.

So we became friends. I'd make up the games and she'd just go along with whatever. And I would tell her stories on our walks home from school – I was a storyteller even then. Appollonia of course enjoyed being entertained. Our friendship grew and grew. Then we lost touch for about twenty years. She went her way and I went mine, and isn't that the way it goes, though, so often. With friends.

I bet you can guess how we found each other again! The thing of it is, I only really got on there in the first place to promote my chapbook. You must do that with your press too,

I'm sure. Anyway, do you know what Appollonia said, when she got in touch with me? She said, "This Internet thing is the wave of the future!" I know. Adorable.

The funny thing was, I didn't remember her at first. Her name rang a bell, but it was such a long time ago. So I looked through her friends list to see if I recognized anyone, and of course I saw you, and so many of the other guests here, and I thought, What a small, small world we live in.

Soon after that we met up for lunch and got reacquainted. I took her to that place, what's that place called. You know, the restaurant that's loud, with the salad they make from things that fall out of trees? Anyway, that's where we went. And it all came rushing back to us. Grade school. Playing. Our storytime walks. And I told Appollonia about my chapbook and she said – if you can believe it – "What's a chapbook?" Oh dear. So I explained it to her, and she was thrilled for me and asked me could she buy it in the bookstores, and I said no, she could only buy it directly from me. Poor thing, she has no idea how it all works.

She doesn't know anything about the "scene," either, but I guess why would she? Just because she knows all these people through – How does she know all these people? She's really kept that to herself. Although she's never even heard of sp@cebar, which is amazing to me. To be that out of touch with what's going on in the world. You put out his last flipbook, didn't you? She said to me, "Well, what does he do?" And I said, "He engages with the absence of sound. He communicates his poetry through gestures and facial expressions." And she said – now, you'll get a real kick out of this – "Isn't that what a mime clown does?" I said to her, "Appollonia, sp@cebar is not a mime clown. He is a soundless poet." She really doesn't have a clue. I mean, I've never seen one of his performances, but at least I know. You know?

Appollonia is an accountant now, and she's married to a man named Bob, who's in one of the trades, I can't remember which, and they've talked about children and they just bought a condo, but not a loft condo, it's one of those postage-stamp, cookie-cutter high-rise ones, which she is going to have a very hard time selling, but still, it's property, and you've got to believe that owning any property in the city is an achievement these days. I said that to her too, and she said, "Do you really think it'll be hard to sell?" I said, "Appollonia, none of us has a crystal ball." Well, maybe some of us do. Appollonia's parents might! But anyway, I said she should be proud of her accomplishments.

And she's going to be a mother someday! Which is the last thing I'd want to be, but who am I to judge? The second-last thing I'd want to be is a homeowner. The Appollonias of the world are welcome to it. I explained to her that renting is the way to go if you're an artist, and I told her, "Appollonia, you are so lucky you're not a creative person. You are so free!" And do you know what she said to me? She said, "Well, yeah, it's true, I guess I am pretty lucky that way. None of those pesky thought bubbles overhead to weigh down my empty noggin!" I'm telling you, she says things like that all the time! It's hilarious. But of course also very sad.

The thing about me is, I think about other people. Other people are always at the forefront of my mind. And I worry about Appollonia, I really do. She's a bit of a loner, so she's not the best with crowds, which is why I said I'd come with her tonight and keep her company. Okay, I'll come clean and admit that there are people at this party who I would like to meet, of course there's that. But really I am here for Appollonia.

I wasn't even going to come over here, but Appollonia said I should. One of her favourite sayings is, "Why not go out on a limb, because that's where the fruit is." Priceless, I know. That's what she said to me earlier, when I happened to mention that it might be nice to talk to you about my chapbook and about poetry in general. So here I am.

There are people who might say to me, "What are you doing with a person like Appollonia?" And I would say to those people, "Hold on, back up, please. Appollonia is my friend. Don't tell me what she's like – I know what she's like. But she is my friend who I care for very deeply." That's what I would say.

You know, I'm so glad I met you, you're so easy to talk with. And you're enjoying the pie too, I see! Oh, I'm sorry. Strudel. And here I thought it was pie all this time. Now isn't that funny, because I'm normally very observant. I can even show you right here in my chapbook, it has all these observations I make every day, transformed into verse. I've got this acrostic series on yearning, let me just find that page . . . You do? No, no, of course, I know how it goes. You've got people you need to – sure. It's a party! I really should be getting back to Appollonia, anyway, she's starting to look pretty lonely over there. You mean that's where you were – Well, perfect, the three of us, then! Oh. Really? No, sure, I understand completely, I don't mind at all. I was just on my way to the bathroom, anyway. Where is the bathroom, do you know? Of course you'd know. Could you please just point me in the right direction before you – You don't know? Well, that's fine. I'll find my way there eventually.

JAY BROWN

THE GIRL FROM THE WAR

This happened twelve years ago, when Kevin Lock came home from his time in Nepal. It was the late fall in 1996, before Oscar was born and before we'd moved into the old farmhouse in Watertown. We lived in Toronto, in a yellow one-bedroom apartment on Vermont Avenue. Kendra worked Thursday through Monday at her parents' restaurant, C'est Ça, and I had a contract with a company that provided special effects for the film industry. Kendra was pregnant and we'd decided to keep the baby, so we were saving as much as we could. I was working nights and she worked days, and our conversations in the rare hours we spent together tended to bleed into real estate and money-market accounts, practical matters pertaining to the near and middle future.

Kendra was halfway through a degree in horticulture and envisioned a family business selling fresh herbs directly to Toronto's restaurant industry: trays of Genovese basil, tarragon, oregano, chervil. She spent a lot of time thinking about the way this could work. As she saw it, we'd need greenhouses and at least two acres of land somewhere close to the city. She'd already designed a logo for the door of the delivery van: the silhouette of a mint plant and a line of ants carrying pieces of its leaves away. I didn't have a counter dream of my own with that same degree of specificity, so I went along with hers.

"Although, why does it have to be ants?" I said.

"Because that's something that ants do."

"People will think we're exterminators."

"No, they won't. They'll be happy little insects, not menacing ones."

"Oh. Well, then, why not ladybugs? I've always been kind of afraid of ants."

"You're afraid of everything," she sighed. "You're afraid of driving and . . . magic markers . . . and . . ."

". . . and little electric carpet shocks. And fog." Our lives were strained and whatever the topic was it always felt like we were one breath away from some manic argument. Kendra had a way of taking playful facts about me and spinning them into small humiliations. I tried to keep it light. "It's true. And monkeys! Do you think there's a word for all of those? Monkaphobia? Carpetricobia?"

She laughed dutifully, but I'd lost her. She wanted to talk about our future home, about kitchen stoves, a cast-iron super-efficient monster we could eventually have imported from Scandinavia. It would heat the house. A big investment up front, she said, but it would pay off down the road.

Kendra has great big curls – almost ringlets – and back then she mostly wore them wrapped in a bun, an expertly spun and folded package held tightly together with a single elastic. Her fingers were forever searching out zany stray curls and tucking them back into the knot. I liked the solid feel of the knot, the cloud of her hair concentrated like that. I used to bite it or squeeze it like a stress ball. Sometimes when I touched her she'd take over, grabbing my hand and using it like a puppet to stroke her own skin. My fingers hung limply in her grip and grazed the light hairs all along her forearm.

The production I was working on was called *Blue Hawk*, a mini-series set in the late eighteenth century about conflict between a Native village and a British outpost in northern Ontario. Blue Hawk was the main character. He was some kind of double agent for the Cree. We'd never see the final product since the primary market was German television and the whole thing was being dubbed then shipped off overseas. They'd dressed one corner of the facilities at the old Gooderham & Worts distillery to look like the mud and timber of a military fort.

The current episode called for ice on the laneways, so the characters could skate from building to building, as if that's how garrisoned British military got around back then. But the producers hadn't anticipated that the December weather in Toronto wouldn't be cold enough to keep ice frozen during the day when they needed it. They decided that they'd build up as much ice as they could in the nights, which dipped below zero just long enough for freezing to occur, and then start shooting the skating scenes at first light for as long as they could. My job was to renew the ice every night by misting the cobblestone laneways with water that then froze into hard, thin layers like candy. My partner, Joe Cicone, started at one end of the plant and I started at another. We were the only ones on the entire lot. Every half hour or so we'd see each other, have a few quick words, and then turn around and paint another layer.

I had trouble explaining why to Kendra, but in some ways that was the best job I'd had in my life. The traffic on the nearby Gardiner Expressway slowed to the occasional delivery van and airport shuttle. The streetlights flashed their colours into empty streets – you could hear their internal clicks over the hissing of the hose. They were the loudest things in a sleeping city. The nights were calm but it was the activity that I liked most of all. It wasn't drudgery. I was focused and appreciative. The water was too warm coming out of the hose, and too much of it at once could quickly ruin an hour of work by melting the ice. It had to rain down in a plume loose enough to cool before it landed. I applied the layers with a passion so guarded against over-enthusiasm and yet so fed by desperation against the coming of the day that in the narrow channel between these two feelings, something tingled in me all night long. It was wonderful and terrible, akin, in a way, to sexual pleasure. The ice accumulated like tree rings, each blanketing the other with surety and fastness – a molecular perfection.

The last night of the job was a Wednesday and so we finished up on Thursday morning as the sleepy camera and lighting men arrived and began unloading their gear from a truck. After we'd coiled our hoses into their muddy bins it was eight-thirty and we flipped a coin. Joe lost and drove the truck back to the lockup on Cherry Street and I went to C'est Ça to say hello to Kendra before going home and to bed.

I came in the back door and found her helping Kumar, the chef, by sprinkling a row of plated omelettes with chopped green onion. I slipped behind her and slid one hand under the strap of her apron, where her shirt was warm and moist. She batted me away.

"We're packed," she said. "Are your hands clean? Can you take these to the Germans, the table of four, in the window booth?" She held the plates out to me and mouthed a silent "please."

At the table, the Germans all turned to me with big smiles. There were four of them, two older couples, and they were in great moods. They were laughing about the warm December.

"How will you play hockey?" said one man with a healthy head of grey hair brushed up into one compact wave. "Where is this Canadian winter? We brought boots, but where is all the ice and snow?"

"In Germany," said a woman I presumed to be his wife, "we have our gardens all covered in snow right now. We are stealing from you," she laughed.

Kendra came out of the kitchen and edged past me on her way to another table. She had her apron tied up high, under her chest, and her pregnancy was just showing, I now saw. She looked frazzled and somewhat angry under her armfuls of pancakes, strangely unlovely and unfamiliar against C'est Ça's faux-aged yellow walls.

I turned back to the Germans and was distracted by the front page of the newspaper that one of the women had been reading, which was folded in half in the middle of the table. The intriguingly large, bold font headline drowned out the photo it addressed, the way big events often will, and I wondered about it.

"Yitzhak Rabin was assassinated," said the woman in answer to my peering. "Isn't it so terrible?" The rest of the table nodded their heads in agreement. She unfolded the paper and held the photo up so I could see it. Rabin's legs were on the ground, while all around him other men in dark suits were about to spring into action.

There was a weird space into which rushed the ability of water to freeze, the need for breakfast, and the sharing of this largish piece of world news. I was taken by a sudden force of emotion birthing from me like an alien clawing through my stomach. I almost broke down right there, cried in the morning in front of the Germans. They could see I was upset, presumably by the news, and were all made a little awkward by it; after all, what did these strangers really know about me? Maybe I felt deeply involved in the Jewish homeland. Maybe I was prone to tears. The truth is I didn't know what upset me so much about it. I really only barely knew who Yitzhak Rabin was, so there was no reason to be upset, but something inside had found its flimsy key. The low orange light of the new sun caught all of the imperfections in the grain of the table, and I tried to focus on them to compose myself: the scratches and the bits of salt and sugar and crumbs. I felt unexpectedly lost or as if I had lost something.

I went back into the kitchen and kept on going, out the back door that led into the courtyard. There was a large water tank in the rear of the restaurant that shaded a bit of lawn. I could see a slice of the glowing street through a passage onto the sidewalk, where the blacktop had just started to steam away the night's freeze accumulation, but in the dark yard the grass was still battered in a frost so thick it snapped under my shoes.

"What are you doing?" It was Kendra, half annoyed, half concerned, hanging her head out of the steaming door.

"Nothing." I turned away from her so that I was facing the wall. I needed to be alone.

I heard the crunch of her footsteps coming towards me. Then she stopped and stood right behind me, a question in her silence.

"What is it?"

I kept my face away, but she'd know anyway. "Give me a minute."

Her warm hand on the back of my neck, curious, but protective and reassuring. Her lips and a kids' joke close to my ear. "What did the Englishman say to the two-headed giant?"

"I'm twenty-eight years old," I said. Too old and too young.

"'Ello 'ello."

The following Sunday there was a message from Kevin Lock on our answering machine, inviting me and Kendra to a slide show in the basement of his grandmother's house in Millgrove Township. Kevin had been away for almost a year, first in India and later in Nepal. Kendra was reluctant to commit. C'est Ça was closed on Sundays and we generally had dinner with her parents on that night. Plus she wouldn't know anyone and she wasn't able to drink. She'd met Kevin once or twice when we'd first gotten together, when my old tribe was less scattered than it was now, but she might feel like a stranger, she said. I secretly hoped she'd stay behind.

"Does it matter to you if I come?" she asked me.

"Of course it matters."

Kevin's parents had both died in a car accident when we were kids and he moved to Millgrove after that, to live with his grandparents, but he kept going to school in Hamilton.

He took the Greyhound back and forth, like an adult. Sleepovers at his house were as good as visiting the moon. His grandparents lived on a small acreage surrounded by potato farms, a fifteen-minute walk from where the bus let us off on the highway. Things that were unthinkable in the city were routine here: hundreds of newts rising and sinking in the cavern of a flooded culvert, the yipping of coyotes at night, and the sense, really, that just beyond the trees at the end of the farm across from Kevin's place – the furthest we could see from his bedroom window – was a gasping wilderness where feral dogs ran down unfortunate wanderers and chewed them into unrecognizable piles of bone and hair.

We'd stayed friends through high school and university, but it was those mornings, always winter in my mind, which were the zenith of our time together. At least that's how it is looking back on it. The line that Kevin lived on was gravel and the snow accumulated in bowed drifts on both sides of it. The wind coming off the fields was bitterly cold and I'd wrap my scarf around my face, breathing through the damp weave of the wool. At the end was the warmth of the bus, and all of those grown-ups facing forwards. We'd take our seats and the driver would pull away from the slushy curb where we'd been waiting. He'd always say, where will it be today, boys? New York, sir. Africa, sir. Atlantis, sir.

We arrived late and rang the doorbell at Kevin's grandmother's house in twilight. Kevin was at least ten pounds lighter, had the drawn look of someone just recovered from an illness. His hair was long and he wore a thick shirt open at the neck, a loose string of yellow beads prominently dangling. He said hello to us at the door, kissing Kendra on both cheeks and taking my outstretched hand and holding it between both of his in welcome. He'd been to eastern monasteries and he had the hat to prove it.

"I thought Buddha would be fatter," Kendra whispered to me when we were all settled in the darkened basement.

"He's sucking it in," I said. Whoever else could make it was there. Peter Bell was with a man I didn't know. Calvin May was stretched out regally, occupying an entire sofa by himself. Kevin's younger brother Robbie had graduated high school in the spring and still lived with Granny Lock. Since he'd been only four when his parents died, Robbie had simply gone to the local Millgrove schools his whole life. He was pure Millgrove. He had bad skin and lumbered around in long hair and a rasta tam with a resigned and crazy authority.

At the back of the room, manning the projector, was Ajla, the woman Kevin had brought back with him from Nepal. Though there was a fire in the woodstove and the basement was very warm, Ajla was wearing an elfish woollen hat with beaded flaps flipped up from her ears and a bent Suessian peak. She'd wedged her long body yogi-like behind a table in the rear of the room. The cord for the slide projector disappeared under her legs and arms, compacted into a knot under the table. She watched the proceedings with eyes so soporifically heavy and unblinking that she seemed to be sleeping with eyes open until Kevin asked her for a new slide and apparently without movement the machine was engaged and the picture advanced.

Kevin stood at the front, beside the images projected on the white wall and narrated through a series of photographs. "There," he said – and the shadow of his unwavering finger hung across a white sweep of mountain. "This is taken from halfway up the pass and the little blur here is a cow who'd hurt its leg. The shepherds were leaving it behind but tying prayer flags to its tail to keep predators away. It was just being tortured by the dogs nipping at it while it hobbled around."

"I could ea-ea-eat a fuh-fucking cow at the present moment," said Robbie Lock. "That I could do."

"Quiet, Robbie," said Kevin.

"Yes, put a sock in it, Robbie. Filthy," said Granny Lock.

Granny Lock's yellow mutt, Sam, was parked between Robbie's thighs with a nose up on his lap and Robbie was digging ferociously into the fur behind his head then rolling Sam's long, soft ears up and down with his fingers.

The slide machine rolled forward and forward and forward.

"This is the Abeneri step well in Rajasthan . . ."

"This is the restaurant at the Bharatpur Bird Sanctuary . . ."

"This is a group of men gathered around an asphalt cutter in Kathmandu . . ."

"And this is the gompa at the Root Institute in Dharamsala, about a week before His Holiness the Karmapa Lama arrived. This is where we lived for eight weeks."

Kevin's voice took on an annoying tone, soggily nostalgic as if stunned with beatitude. The term "His Holiness" hung unnaturally in the air like a puff of burnt kitchen grease.

"I could eat a fucking asphalt cutter."

"Robbie!"

Kendra grumbled beside me.

There was a soft "huh" noise from the back of the room – like a suppressed sneeze – and the woman, Ajla, shifted in her position behind the slide machine.

"Press the button again, Aj'?"

Calvin May, for sure, but the rest of us also, snuck glances at Ajla when we could. Because there was more to her than just a trip to Nepal. She'd been in Dubrovnik when the Serbs laid siege and had been smuggled out by boat, bereft of everything but a bundle of money stitched into the sole of her shoe and her father's platinum cufflinks in her stomach. So Kevin's letter had said. She'd seen terrible things. Her body was scarred. There was a pink ridge riding up from the back of her neck like two lines of plasticine pressed together. I wondered if this continued up into her scalp and interrupted the growth of hair there and so she was shy to go hatless. She was a real live girl from the war.

"So this is Kopan abbey," said Kevin and paused. The photo was of an ugly wall with several westerners dressed incongruously in the saffron robes of Buddhist monks and posing for the camera. There was a sign in the centre of the shot, a painted board that said, "Kindly refrain from killing stealing lying sexual contact and intoxicants."

"We all took turns washing dishes."

I remembered Kevin's bed in grade seven – so stocked with pornography under the mattress that it had a noticeable arch. And his condom stealing pathology – the arms and legs of his grade six graduation suit puffed with hundreds of Trojans and Durex Superthins bound to live out their lonely years and expire in Kevin's dark closet.

"We were here for three months. It changed my life. It really did."

Afterwards, we wandered around the living room eating sliced gouda on pumpernickel squares and drinking whatever there was to drink. Peter Bell made strange small talk, quickly excused himself, and drove off with the man he had come with, back to his condominium in Toronto. "What happened to Peter?" Calvin said to me. "You'd think he was the boss at an office mingler – and since when is he so out?"

I shook my head.

"He's a prick," said Calvin. "He's always been a prick – he's just a rich homo prick now."

Kendra had settled into a sofa with her ginger ale and I glanced at her, made a show of rolling my eyes. We were having a silent war over the drink in my hand. She was irritated that she couldn't and I could – that she was talking strollers with Granny Lock while I was being an asshole with Calvin May.

"The problem with Peter," continued Calvin, "is that he's not creative enough to enjoy his money. He's rigid in his thinking. He knows everything there is to know about tax law but he learned everything else about life from men's fashion magazines. And you," Calvin poked a finger into my chest, "are no fucking better."

"What?"

"God, man, the first time I've seen you out of the house in five months is at a freaking slide show. There's not even a child yet. You're deteriorating. You're whacking off to Ikea catalogues."

"Keep it down." Calvin, drunk even before the first slide had been cast on the wall, was flinging arcs of saliva as he spoke.

He complied by draping an arm over my shoulder and steering us both to face the large picture window that looked over the farm next door but was now more a mirror on the living room. It was snowing lightly against the pane and so on us too, me and my friends, Robbie at the counter with a sloshing mug of pilfered Tio Pepe, Kevin and Kendra now on the couch behind a two-foot stack of photographs. Everyone there but everyone sitting also in the dim stubble of a corn field and paying no heed to the snow whirling all about us.

"You know," said Calvin, "I always thought the first one of us to have a kid, do a wedding, would be Kevin, and look what he's done. Ajla – did you see her slink off to the bedroom?"

Ajla had disappeared into Kevin's bedroom immediately following the slide show and hadn't come back out.

"She doesn't speak, you know. She barely seems to move – just glides around one plane higher than everyone else."

"Oh, come on, Calvin. She's been through hell."

"I know. I know it. The real deal."

"It's a Buddhist thing – a sort of vow of silence, or maybe between the bombs and the death, the gong ringing in the mountains, and then finding herself parked in front of a plate of fresh scones in a basement with a bunch of twits like you, she's simply shell-shocked."

"'Simply shell-shocked,'" Calvin mocked. He closed his eyes a moment and they circled up slowly in their purple sockets when they reopened. Calvin's vaporous breath washed over me.

"Since when does Kevin give two shits about the Dalai Lama and his furry hat? It's a fucking set-up – he's done it to get into her pants. That scar must slip around her body like a freaking piece of lace. Kevin Lock. She doesn't know Kevin Lock. Imagine. Lodged with her in a rocky monastery in the mountains. The whole thing gives me a hard-on of sesquipedalian proportions."

"You incredible pig."

"What? Me? You're forgetting yourself. Who blew the hundred dollars his grandmother gave him on lap dances at O'Doul's? Who kept Tammy Summers's panties in a box in his sock drawer until he was nearly twenty? Will no one," said Calvin, spinning around to face the room, "join me in a toast to the original pig and the Karmapa Lama?"

Robbie, from behind the sofa: "To the pa-pa-pa pig!"

Calvin passed out early on the couch in the basement and Granny Lock booted Robbie from his room so Kendra and I could spend the night. At eleven-thirty there was only me and Kevin and Granny Lock sitting around the table in the kitchen. Granny and I were polishing off the last of the sherry, but not Kevin – who said he'd sworn off booze for good in Nepal. He was doing the dishes.

"Isn't that astonishing?" said Granny, clearly not buying it.

"I haven't had a drink in seven months."

Granny shot me a look.

"It's the truth."

Kevin's sobriety was especially irritating under the kitchen's blueing fluorescents. I wanted us to be in the living room, looking over the empty field.

"Remember," I said, "those times, when we'd flood the garden over in the winter and we'd play shinny on the weekends with your neighbours? Piping Whitesnake out the window on a ghetto blaster."

"Sure, yeah, of course," joined Kevin, "Blasting Whitesnake with the Bevinses. But that was just that one year."

"No. It feels like it was forever – like it was a whole world of time."

"That's the way of things."

"Come on."

"When Ajla and I went to an initiation in Dharamsala, His Holiness . . ."

"I have to tell you, Kev," I said, "I can't get used to this."

"Well, it was very atmospheric. There were thousands of monks gathered on a field – and the rain and lammergeiers circling overhead in the greyness for hours. You have to imagine it. We ate under flapping plastic tarps and the great birds landed and pecked around us like geese. His Holiness forgot some of the items he needed for the ceremony – a scarf and a box – but he continued with the initiation without them. Someone asked him afterwards what was going to become of the traditions of Buddhism if we stopped valuing the old ways of doing things in favour of a more Western, easygoing kind of approach."

"Don't say 'His Holiness.'"

"He said everything was going to disappear. Buddhism would be reduced to its most basic truths – emptiness and compassion."

"What the hell does that mean?"

"'The greatest medicine is the emptiness of everything.'"

"What does it mean? Sounds canned. Sounds self-help. Sounds B.S."

I blew air through my fist like a trumpet – "Do dooo doo doooo!" – wanting to get a rise out of Kevin.

"But I feel it. I know how it sounds. But it isn't canned if you feel it." Kevin hung the tea towel neatly over the loop on the oven door. "It's a decision to feel it. That's the thing. There's no getting around it. You just decide. Ajla calls it surrendering."

He swept his hair up then into a broom on the top of his head. It stuck straight up into the air and made his face even longer and thinner than it already was. If Granny Lock hadn't been with us at the table I would have punched him in the stomach and rolled him out the back door into the snow.

The night after Yitzhak Rabin was assassinated I found myself on the bad porch of an old friend's childhood home. I'd stolen a cigarette from Robbie's jacket in the closet. Glorious night – the moon full, or nearly, and the fresh snow glowing in the cups of every leaf it could find. I was drunk and painting swirls in the snow that had fallen onto the wooden railing. Years ago, I'd helped Kevin and his grandfather lay flagstones at the head of the laneway, at the approach to the stairs. There was a kind of lichen that had grown in the tiny shallows between the set stones. When I walked down onto it, little rhyzomatic tufts crunched slightly under my shoes, and I paced back and forth, thrilling in the soft sound of it.

Everyone knows that anyone can go anywhere they want, can leave or turn around or wait as they wish. A thousand little commitments make it feel impossible but it's not, and I was playing drunken dare games with myself on this theme. Walking one step then another out towards the laneway tunnelled by giant windbreak spruce on either side.

I'd only just reached the drive when I heard a sound and there was Sam, one leg up and urinating on the woodpile. A way off there was a slim shadow against the snowy field, waiting on Sam and smoking quietly, like me. Neither of them had heard me, and after Sam had finished his business Ajla began slowly walking out into the frozen cornfield, Sam reluctantly following.

Though I was hidden, I yelled after her, emerging from the lane in my drunken stumbles. I thought how maybe this would remind her of something horrible following her through a different night. I knew it before I even did it, cruel in the name of curiosity.

But she wasn't afraid of me – only sized me up and said nothing. As inside I thought she looked overdressed for the warmth, outside she wore nothing more than the same thin sweater and hat.

"In the summertime," I said, "You should see this in the summertime. I mean it's just wild with fireflies. In June . . . We never even said hello, back at the place there."

She opened her mouth a fraction and pointed into it, shaking her head.

"Right." We were walking now out into the field, Sam exactly one foot from my heel. The corn was long harvested but there were still rows of thick yellow stalks tipped against each other like broken fences every four feet. "Does it feel to you like we're the last soldiers on the battlefield? Sorry. Drunk."

We reached the hub of an ancient tractor wheel she'd been aiming for and sat down on the treads of cracked rubber.

"I've got a memory of those fireflies like you wouldn't believe. There're so many of them in June – so much light you think it would be noisy." Which is how it had been, at least, half a lifetime ago, when I'd half believed that firefly light really was the flickering lamp-shine of some otherworldly place. "I'm sorry, you know; I'm sorry if I scared you back there. I don't think I did but you know, if . . . And for being so drunk and stupid. You must already hate Kevin's friends."

Sam had settled himself in front of me – looking uncomfortable on the hard ground – and was aggressively shoving his head between my hands and my thigh. "What are you doing, Sam? Go find some rotten meat. Go snuffle."

Besides pointing to her mouth, Ajla hadn't communicated anything at all that indicated her feelings about my company. I'd just followed her, like Sam. And she looked at me when I spoke the way I looked at Sam when he barked. Which is to say, aware of me, but entirely unconcerned with what I was trying to say. But now she pointed behind me and up, and I turned.

There was weather in the sky, a razor-straight line of cloud advancing from the glow of Hamilton and the east. It appeared as a blackness that erased the stars, which then shone along the entire front as the moon spread its light while being eaten, like a burst balloon of white. She'd seen terrible things.

"That's beautiful, isn't it? It doesn't matter who you are. The sultan of Brunei gets the same moon as everybody else."

She was smiling when I said that. The vacancy of her face dissolved and her lips came to a point and opened when she smiled – the darkness of that mouth, her ruined teeth.

"Doesn't it feel like we're on the verge of huge change? Everything is mixing together. And it's all happening and it's all too late."

She nodded and I kissed her, felt the inside of her mouth and the sharp points of a scar where her tongue had been. I didn't open my eyes. I felt lightning tremble in my core. I kept jabbing at her ruin, compelled and titillated. How full she must have been. And with what purpose? I held her close and wouldn't let her go. I was stuck. She made a quick movement and then there was a noise so wild I thought for a moment something had attacked the dog – a panicked and feral sound of scary urgency and a twist and I was on my back behind the tire. Ajla ran through the field towards the house. Sam barked after her, then turned, confused.

"I made a mistake!" I yelled. "Please, I made a mistake!"

A distant tapping announced her rush up the front stairs and inside. One hundred metres from where I sat the windows of the house glowed tiny and yellow, like a match taking refuge under a tin thimble, or like a pizza joint at four in the morning. I felt the way a shooting star might feel when it finally sees where it's going to land. It was too late to change my mind. At the time it wasn't what I wanted. The blast was over and I couldn't see anything waiting for me but one long dying note. I wasn't ready to come in from outside, but there was nowhere else to go.

FRAN KIMMEL

LAUNDRY DAY

When Harvey walked out last summer he said he was never coming back. Now he says he'll be home tomorrow so we can be together for Jesus's birthday. Harvey drives the long haul trucks. I'm supposed to put on my red dress and we're gonna go dancing. He'll be some pissed if he wakes up to a pile of dog hair on his pillow on Christmas morning, which is the big reason I'm at the Soap 'n Suds on the coldest day of the year, running everything I own through the heavy-duty cycle.

Molly says I can't take care of a cabbage, and I should thank the gods he's changed his mind. But when Harvey disappeared, I got nails that grew shiny white at the tips and didn't splinter to bits at the first sign of trouble. And I got a dog. During those first long nights, I curled around his tiny body in the dark. When his little chest thumped and quivered, I held him close to my heart and could feel his hot breath on my palm. I didn't think once about rolling over and crushing him to death – what used to scare me into sitting straight up whenever I dreamed of babies of my own.

When Molly met Max the first time she said, *Gracie, you must be dumber than a bag of rocks.* She said Maxine was a girl's name, and I had no business getting a dog when I couldn't tell he was a boy and couldn't pay the bills. *And just look at his paws,* she yelled as she waltzed out my door. *He'll be big as an elephant.*

I asked Joe in produce if I should change Maxine's name. Joe's real smart and votes in all the elections. He rattled off a dozen famous Maxes – kings and warriors and artists and such – so now whenever my sister comes around, I hide all the pricey toys and say, *Good dog, Max*, when he drops my shoe or stops chewing on the TV cord.

I got three washers going in a row. Seems I'm the only one with dirty laundry in this town, except now there's a young girl who's pulled up in front of the window and is wrenching her boy from the back seat and dragging her green garbage bag along the crusty snow, and now the boy's inside and mom's yanking his arms out of his coat. She looks like she's mad. He's got a cough that doesn't sound too good, but I think at least she didn't leave him in the car.

Oprah showed about a lady who said she was the most hated woman in America 'cause she forgot about her baby girl in the back seat all day and that poor baby fried to death. That lady was real smart, too. A principal. The lady's husband usually did the drop-off but he was getting his tooth yanked. So she bought doughnuts for the teachers and jumped out of the car all excited and didn't look back and just sailed around greeting everyone and asking about their summer 'cause it was the first day of school. Harvey says I'm too stupid to have kids and raise 'em right. I don't hate that poor lady no matter if the whole world turns its back on her. But I do know something. If I ever was a momma, I'd sure as eggs never forget it.

When Harvey called on Halloween night from somewhere between Seattle and Spokane, his voice sounded soft and low and not at all like I remembered. He said he was alone in his truck, but I thought I heard her breathy sleep in the background. He'd been praying over me a lot, he said. Reading his Bible about how woman was created out of Adam in order to be his helper, and when women rebel against their God-assigned role, they sin. He said if I could try a little harder he would let bygones be bygones, and I was lucky he never pressed charges, and he was thinking of taking me back. He said other stuff I didn't hear so good cause there were pirates and tooth fairies yelling for candy at my door and holding out plastic pumpkins. Max was scared to death of the commotion, so I put him in my bedroom with his teddy and a rawhide. I think Harvey mighta said he missed my tuna casserole.

I didn't tell Harvey that I hadn't prayed once since he left or about how I got a job at Bing's Grocery. And I sure didn't tell him about Max. Every time I put on the ugly brown shirt and orange tie and *Be Patient – Trainee* button, a combo what took four hours bagging groceries to pay off, Max's ears go down and his eyes look watery. Joe says split shifts were invented to keep the money-grubbing capitalists from paying for breaks, but I say thank heavens for capitalists then. Max can't hold it past four hours. During our first weeks together, Max spent his alone time digging a football-sized crater through the drywall by the back door. He musta thought that kitchen wall was all that stood between us. He didn't care if he broke every nail just to find me again. I'd run all the way home on my breaks and snap on Max's leash, and he'd drag me around the thistle field until I thought my arm might break, which wouldn't be the first time.

That girl has crammed everything into one load and she's put her coughing boy on a blanket on the sorting table. He just lays there, feebly grabbing at sunbeams with his stubby fingers. I'm sitting right in front of her on my plastic chair, but she won't look at me, and neither does the boy, and I don't want to stare, but she has the prettiest nails I've ever seen, flowers painted on her thumbs with a blue sapphire on the petal.

Now that I got nails of my own, I pay more attention to everybody else's. You need a special contraption for clipping dog's nails that looks like an eyelash curler. Max hates getting his nails done, but if he gives in to his fears he could be tearing through the field one day and a nail might rip at the root, which is exactly how those torturers in cement rooms get their torturees to confess to crimes they didn't even know how to imagine.

I'm still trying to get the hang of the Shimmering French Manicure. I can't get the white half moons to look the same on each finger. The kit comes with tiny curved strips for guides, but they don't stick straight, and fall off at all the wrong times, like when you're sweeping the polish in a single even stroke. Max makes a huge scene when it's his turn, squirming and moaning, but when we're finished he forgets he was scared and sits like an angel and slobbers on the linoleum while I fish out his Milk-Bone from the jar.

Dogs grow new coats when it's winter, which leaves their old coats in your cereal bowl and your underwear drawer. Harvey called on Remembrance Day night when I was sweeping up dog hair by the bag load. I remember 'cause that same morning Bing went over the loudspeaker to announce a moment of silence for the fallen soldiers. Nobody knew whether to stand at attention behind their carts or keep pushing down the aisle with their heads bowed. Harvey said he was hauling steel to New Orleans, a godless cesspool in his opinion, a place where police fired seven hundred rounds into the air – *kaboom, kaboom* – just to see who'd call in, and nobody did. I'm not surprised. Deafness comes with an on-off switch, otherwise we'd go crazy listening to what we're not meant to hear – all that thudding and cracking and pleading. Harvey asked if I'd given any thought to our last conversation. I shrugged, rubbing the fuzzy red poppy in my pocket, which of course he couldn't see. If his question was something he thought to test me with, he couldn't wait for my answer. He said he'd done a lot more praying on the road and that God kept steering him towards forgiveness. Forgiveness for what? My flinging a mayonnaise jar at his head? Though, I did crack him pretty good and he probably shoulda got stitches, his turn for once. He said he'd been picturing goin' dancing with me in my red dress. I closed my eyes and thought about swaying against him with the lights down low and his hands on my breasts, digging into them with his fingertips. How he would moan and tell me how fine I was.

It's blue cold outside. The girl must have chose regular instead of heavy duty, cause our wash cycles finish at exactly the same time. Her boy is asleep on the sorting table, lips bubbling, legs and arms spread like a biology frog. We carry our loads to our dryers, wet sleeves and legs dangling. Once the tumbling starts, the window gets steamy enough to write our names. The radio guy says to expect cold and more cold, snow and more snow. I'll be out there soon enough, hunkered down low like Santa Claus, sack strapped to my sleigh, waving my mittens like windshield wipers so I can see what's ahead and don't fall sideways and get swallowed by a drift. I got to work a second shift tonight. Though I imagine in this storm the store will be empty as a ghost town. Bing says people need bread even when the sky is falling, and it's the grocers that shine a beacon of light. Joe says we should get danger pay if we gotta be shining our beacons in a minus-forty degrees windchill.

Molly says when Harvey gets home he'll tie Max out back where he belongs. I think about Max all alone shivering in the wind, like the big yellow dog that lives down the alley. That dog paces back and forth in his empty cage, nothing but a frozen water dish for company. When I trudge past him on my way to work he throws his great paws up on the fence and whimpers the same trembling note over and over, and I fish out a treat from my pocket, and he wolfs it down in one gulp and licks my fingers like an apology. Then I tell him I have to go. I try to pat his great head through the cold steel. He stays at that fence and stares after me, and no matter how many times I turn back, he's still staring. I know he's a dog and it's not the same as forgetting your baby in the back seat, but it's not that different either. When I try telling Molly that, she says I fell off the beer truck. *Harvey hates dogs. Harvey's allergic. For once in your life, get your head on straight and do the right thing, Gracie.* She reminds me that Harvey likes dancing. *What more do you want*, she asks.

I don't know. More.

I used to watch *Fear Factor* before Max came along. I liked to pretend it was me on the edge looking down. Me slithering through the black tunnel on my stomach, or laying on a bed of snakes, or letting the spiders crawl down my shirt. But I've been thinking more and more lately, what's the point of being brave if it lacks practicality? When I said this to Joe in the lunchroom, he stared at me so hard I felt my underarms get wet. Then he finally said, "It's not spiders and snakes make you brave, Gracie. It's this!" He flung his arm in the air. "Bagging groceries all day in that sappy uniform, getting shin splints from standing so long, coming home half froze but heading right back out because your dog's been waiting." I don't know how Joe knows what he knows, but I felt like he'd crawled up inside me and grabbed hold of my heart.

Harvey says I can expect him tomorrow, and he'll take care of business. I hate that red dress. My boobs won't stay put. I feel like a slut who's trying too hard.

My panties and leggings go round and round. I stare so long at the jumbled, tumbling mess of black and blue that I think it's my eyes staring back at me. I think I can see the reflection of the girl with the beautiful nails lean over and touch her sleeping boy's cheek with her sapphire thumb. I see Max, his tail thwack, thwack, thwacking as I walk through the door. He's only a dog, but he finds God in me, his love so pure and simple I want to fall to my knees.

For once in your life, do the right thing, Gracie.

How do you? That's what I want to know. Maybe you're supposed to drown out the noise in your head and listen to your heart banging inside its bra cup. Maybe that's all you got worth listening to.

It takes me three tries before I can push away from my plastic chair. I stand over the girl and pretend I don't feel my knees tremble. "Take my stuff," I tell her. "Take it all." I drop the empty sack that held my life at her feet.

Her eyes narrow, she's afraid now too, her mouth a weary O. *What for? What you want?*

I have no right words so I turn away and button my coat and cover my mouth with my scarf. I leave my stuff in the Soap 'n Suds with that girl and her boy, cough-burping in his sleep.

Outside, the bite is a shock, even now, even after weeks of sliding down the throat of winter. I trudge towards home, picturing Max, picturing what the audience would see if we were on TV. Not *Fear Factor.* Something more classy.

First, the path into the woods where the town drops off. A girl and her dog, picking their way blind through the dips and valleys of the frozen deer trails. They struggle to the edge of the clearing, climb out from beneath branches hanging heavy like abandoned white sheets after laundry day.

The rippling silver field stretches to forever in the night. The dog breaks through the drifts, and his strong, young legs run and run and run, and he can't feel the cold, and the girl tries to keep up and not look back, and the pair gets smaller and smaller and smaller until they're nothing but perfect, soundless flecks under the falling sky.

SEYWARD GOODHAND

THE FUR TRADER'S DAUGHTER

For many years we lived on a lake in the woods. The sun rising and falling over a ridge of cedar on the edge of our clearing and a pocket watch my father kept on the mantle were all we knew of time. Once a month we journeyed into town for provisions. The town was an old woman with a thousand eyes. When we walked through her grey, cobbled streets dragging suitcases glutted on pelts and the stiff heads of beasts, she drew her lids shut. I could deduce glowing mirages of interior light through curtained windows, but never the whole, comprehensible outline of a flame or bulb.

The market was always open when we came. My father was a trapper and a taxidermist. It wasn't only savage icons the people craved, wild boar tusk and polar grizzle; they wanted softer fare as well, items imparting luck or wisdom, like rabbit's feet or whole wood owl. They liked to pretend they came from another time and place, so they bought martin tail and ermine snout. Women said they would pluck their brows fine and buy red lipstick to go with their new muff. We sold enough to get by.

I watched the traders in the market and they watched me. Most of them were townspeople and therefore different from my father and I, who had travelled from across a wide space. They hawked striped nylon socks, underwear that said "You'll Love Me for Lunch," and bowls of individually wrapped candy. There was a man who sold cheese and a family that traded in zucchinis no matter what season. Sometimes my father struck up a few cordial words with the butcher. The shoppers interested me most. They formed chaotic clusters around things they wanted, held hands, brushed shoulders, and laughed at jokes their friends made. None of them came too near where I stood because they were afraid of the bees that hovered around gaps in my cloak. Still, I could hear what they thought in grooved echoes we weren't supposed to notice.

"She doesn't look real."

"Too pale, her skin."

"It's like she's his slave. Does he lock her up? Did he burn her?"

"Hey, you," my father turned and spoke if he also heard them. "Keep your chin down and don't look at anyone. Don't give them a reason to look at you."

Speaking was verboten. My father bartered with potential clients and I counted out their change, bagged their boar, antler, or bear claw, and kept my eyes on their pockets.

During one December's journey into town, my father got the flu. By the time we'd set up our stall, hissing fluid steamed from the bottom of his trousers, and he'd wrapped himself in some now unsellable lynx pelts. I watched his mess melting the snow but didn't know whether I found it repulsive or not. He shivered on a stool and looked at me as though I were a fawn who refused to come to the dead mother he'd used to bait a trap. "You're so implacable," he seethed. "You don't care. When I made you I should have used more of my own soul." Finally, he grabbed my arm, even though it cost him all his effort. "Get me some medicine. Don't stray."

Down one of the more frequented back streets, the apothecary's kneeled snug in between a patisserie and a shop where tourists could buy imitation medieval swords. I went there while he watched me, my face passing over windowpanes that revealed nothing. Two dazed and starving drones clung to the back of my hood. It's possible that I lived in all those ancient houses, a vengeful emanation sucking air from between the cracks of broken things. Across the street, a boy wearing a plastic Roman helmet pulled on his mother's hand, pointed in my direction, and waved a pamphlet that advertised nightly ghost tours.

Little bells jangled over the apothecary's door. I braced myself for a surge of warmth, but instead the room was cool and dim as a library of lost scrolls. Air seeped through cracks in the floor, which made it seem as if the whole shop was elevated on stilts as high as the sky. The only other patron was an old woman who wandered across the front counter examining liniment cream. She found the blood pressure monitor and tested herself again and again.

"Is there something I can help you with?"

Although he'd been sitting behind the register, I hadn't seen the tall, elfin man until he spoke. He had a pale, small mouth that reminded me of somewhere I could fold myself away and sleep. A tawny mole cheered his neck, and I moved between it and his lips while the old woman repeated her blood pressure out loud.

"Medicine," I said. "For a man."

Finally he asked, "What kind of man?"

"He has the flu."

The woman prowled closer to us and pretended to read the ingredients on a packet of lozenges. She cleared her throat a number of times while the pharmacist went around a second counter and came back with some nectarine-coloured powder. "You may need to come back for more."

"No. I can only come once."

"In that case, give me a moment."

He walked to a third counter, behind and lower than the second. I glanced up and saw a warren of ledges and shelves that were connected at parallel, perpendicular, and even acute angles. Time flowed in a cool circuit, lost and found itself again in eddies that swirled off the rims of counters. Nobody grabbed the back of my neck, forced me to stare into a triggered leg hold, and asked me to describe what I saw.

The pharmacist returned with a vial of iridescent green foam. "If you mix this with the powder it will turn red and taste like fruit. Keep giving it to him until you see a change."

Later, after my father recovered and we had made our way back to our house on the lake, I stared at my palm, where the pharmacist had given me my change, and found a thin, smooth line, like a kitten's claw mark. His eyes were the watery colour of shore pebbles. My eyes had no colour until I mixed ash into round discs of wax and fastened them on.

One day that spring, I looked up from the raccoon brain on the end of my pliers and saw my father wobbling under the weight of his axe. In another flash of silver he'd righted himself and resumed chopping, but the fact was unmistakable – he had begun to shrink. A few weeks later he met and married his wife. She was a long, German woman named Ilse, beautiful in a flat, angular way, and he adored her. I could understand his loneliness, but his sudden ingratiation to this old-world woman confused me.

A few months before she'd been married to the Algerian baker who owned the patisserie next to the apothecary's. My father stole her with promises of fur. The Algerian tried to win her back with her favourite delectations: ladyfingers, baby delights, grand-mere's thumbs, but she preferred the furs. She loved browns the best: beaver, bear, and even fox, if it had been caught during the transitional period between summer and fall. Our living room became cluttered with mirrors and skins she wanted to try, until it looked like a lady's boudoir in some gothic fairy tale. She delighted in finding new combinations and I think even convinced herself that she was an aspiring stylist, though she lived apart from everything there in the woods. She draped her torso with back and her waist with torso, made little hats out of beaver teeth, and framed the straight bones of her jaw with frenetically combed mink wraps. My father trapped, I gutted, and she brushed and braided the dressed fur, then unbraided it.

A week after their wedding, she waltzed into the skinning shed wearing a wolverine tail, stroked my father's slightly narrower neck as he taught me how to rinse marrow from claw sockets, and sighed, "One day I want you to make me another like this weird girl."

April's abundance was diabetic. Bears travelled from lea to forest to lake, sucking grubs out of mulch and indulging in a sublime wanderlust. My father planted a clot of raspberry bushes outside our kitchen window where the view was good, and of course our fixed-frame hives stood along the back tree line amongst the sunflowers we'd seeded at random to attract bees. At least one bear per season lingered around the honey for too long. My father called these bears Winnies, and he said they yielded the nicest fur. Whereas the berries harassed me with thorns I would only find days later in my cheek or the back of my arm, the hives brought me comfort. It wasn't strange that I'd think of those bees as my oblivious, slavish mothers. Sometimes when the days were long and I'd finished all the tasks he'd set out for me, I stood among the hives. If I stuck my tongue out for long enough, worker bees would land on it – and once the queen!

The mother and her two cubs came for our honey on the rarest day. I'd hung two muskrats in the smoking hut, warmed some red berry compote, and whisked the batter my father and Ilse liked to lick off each other's hands before spooning it into our electric waffle maker. As I set the table, Ilse meandered out of their bedroom wearing one of my father's winter parkas and nothing else. She draped herself over my shoulder and linked one of her feet through my calves.

"Are you joining us for breakfast?" She scraped batter off the side of the bowl and suckled it from under her nail. My father came up behind her, washed, combed, and boyish. "I told you, Ilse. She doesn't eat."

When I stepped outside, I found myself unwatched for the first time in my life. It was then that I realized she divided his attention, if only fractionally. Now he would only be able to notice most of me. A part would become mine to do with what I pleased. So I went to see the bees.

Sunny spotlights riddled through gaps in stagnant clouds. I stood in shade on the far side of a hive and hid from eyes at the window. When I stuck my fingers into comb, barbed sentinels swarmed my hand without laying sting, not because they were sympathetic, but because my attacking limb smelled the same as the hive. I felt sad for these guards who failed their monarch. What can a creature do when the linear drive of its instinct hits an unexplained loop? Those same bees had crafted the material I was made of. They hovered and tasted traces of themselves. Then out of nowhere, three shapes stared out from the border of the tree line. Each time I looked up the shapes were a bit more distinct, until a trio of brown heads poked their noses into the clearing, wondering at how I stood there without showing distress. The mother licked her snout. Her male cub swatted his rumbling stomach and nipped her on the elbow, egging her on, while the other cub, a female, tilted her head to one side, swivelling antennae ears, and listening to the silence of my heart.

After that the bears came three or four times a week. I would have shot them if my father had told me to, but he'd been so preoccupied with Ilse indoors, he hadn't. Instead I watched them play. The cubs climbed trees and dived aboard their mother, who reared onto her hind legs and sent them spinning. Whoever had to wait pounced on its sibling twirling through the air, until the surrounding bramble looked wallpapered with snagged tufts of fur. Each visit they came farther and farther into our clearing, until one day they stood just a few feet from the hives, waiting to see what I would do.

I broke off three pieces of comb and tossed them over.

"Hello," I said. "You're welcome."

The girl cub cantered over to me, stopped, edged a little nearer, and stopped. I pinched off a large hexagon, squeezed the contents into my hands and pressed the wax ball into my forehead. I thought of moulding myself a horn. The cub licked the honey off my palm, and when it was gone she stayed. I scratched the divot between her eyes. She nibbled my thumb. When she got bored she ran back to her brother and bit him in the rear. He peed on her. Their mother sucked on a piece of comb. It was nice.

Three shots sculpted what must have been my happiness into a horrible shape. My father floated out from behind a stack of firewood piled beside the house. Ilse followed in a black and white badger scarf.

"We've been watching you," he said.

"Like a chunk of beef under a deadfall, isn't that the way?"

"Ilse's comparisons aren't exact," he stroked her rump. "Nonetheless it's been fascinating to observe. I never knew you could get so close to anything." My cub had been shot in the leg, and she lay on the ground next to her mother and brother playing dead.

Ilse clapped her hands. "It's like Davey Crocket out here, don't you agree?" She flitted between carcasses and my father without looking at any one thing. "You have to skin them now, helpful girl, before they go sour."

The cub licked her paw.

"Ilse wants a bear rug in front of the fireplace," my father stared at me.

"And two little rug slippers."

He threw his skinning knife at my feet and patted Ilse's back to shush her. When I looked back up at them, the pile of chopped wood they leaned against was at least five inches taller.

"Go," he said. "Start with the little one. That one there." As I knelt down I cupped her head and ran my fingers over her nose so she would know that I loved her. By that evening my father and Ilse were the size of twelve-year-old boys.

They noticed the next morning. When Ilse stepped out of bed into a larger world, she must have felt still drunk from the vats of Malbec they'd engulfed to sweeten dinner's bear stew. Being that my body has never altered in size, I can only imagine what shrinking at that velocity must have felt like. An itchy tingle in the musculature; tightness around the eyes and in the nail beds. When she reached the sliding wainscot that partitioned their room from the hall, she might have thought that she was having a stroke. I imagine her blinking, an adolescent mole whose infant blindness didn't fade.

"Gene!" she screamed.

My father, always up before dawn, still slept. He opened his eyes, saw Ilse splattered against the door like a starfish on tiptoe, and roared, "That girl. She's a curse!"

After their initial panic they spoke in whispers. They must have decided that as I only had an artificial sense of the world anyway, and was more or less forged to obey, the best thing they could do was pretend that nothing had changed. As they marched into the kitchen, hips level with the wall sockets, I was already ladling compote into a freshly whisked batter. Ilse hoisted herself onto her chair and kneeled at the table. When she couldn't reach the butter dish, I walked over from my stool in the corner and moved it closer as though that was a politeness I performed every morning. Aside from the fact that they were now three feet tall, everything was the same.

Occasionally my father turned to glare at me, spooning fruit into his mouth while I stoked the fire through a protective leather drape.

It wasn't long, two days and another ten inches at most, before they hatched a plan to kill me. The afternoon was grey and slow, so I took a lighter into the bathroom and sculpted myself a doe head with a single fang that jutted from my cleft.

"Stop it, stop it now!" Ilse howled when I brought them mugs of ginger beer.

Thinking it was the fang that bothered her, I returned to the bathroom and cleaved my face to look exactly like hers. They were eerily silent as I set down their bowl of nuts. Ilse could have been a tiny, quiver-lipped child. She pulled her knees into her chest and dropped her head down the space between them. Suddenly my father erupted off the settee, grabbed my hips, and plowed me down the hall. "What the hell are you doing?" He pressed me into the wall. "Suddenly playful, are you?" I stared down at the top of his head. The oily, bald circle smelled like a rabbit two hours after dying. He shoved me into the bathroom and slammed the door. "Get yourself back to the way I made you."

After all the crafting and reshaping, I glided into bed and fell into a deep sleep. No image brooded behind my eyes, no image ever does, but I felt a warm nose breathing wetness onto my hand.

In the middle of the night I awoke and discovered that my forehead was strapped to the bed with fishing line. Ilse and my father stood eye level with my toes, holding up a storm lantern they'd smashed apart on one side so the shards of glass looked like little girl teeth. My left foot sat melting in their makeshift oven, held taut with a belt they'd looped round my ankle and were using like an elephant hook.

My father was a master trapper, and I had difficulty tearing out of my snare. Wires wrapped around tacks and pinned to the mattress at crucial geometrical nodes transferred the force of my struggle off the lines and back to my body. I bent my joints, thrashed, snarled, gnawed on wires that cut into my gums. My father tugged on the belt so hard he was standing horizontally off the side of the bed. All the while Ilse yelled, "Shut her! Gene! Shut her noises!"

Eventually, instead of trying to raise myself off the mattress, I attempted to shimmy out from under the wires lengthwise. I'd avoided this manoeuvre because it meant kicking my foot even further into the lantern, which was spitting out constellations of flaming palmitate that hazed the back of Ilse's head, igniting her hair and boring black holes into the skin on her arm. With a yowl, I thrust my leg straight through the blaze and knocked Ilse into the wall. The lantern dropped off my foot and sent currents of molten wax pulsing across the floor.

For a moment midst the fire, I calmed. My father didn't yank on my ankle anymore so much as use it to prop himself off the ground, panting like a mountain climber who'd run out of steam sooner than expected. Ilse screeched in the corner and batted back the blaze with a decorative pillow. The scene must have looked even more terrifying to them than it did to me, given our differences in size.

"Put it out!" my father bellowed.

"How?" I asked.

"That one," he pointed to one of the tacks, which I unpinned. "Now that one." In this way he ciphered my escape. I limped to the bathroom, wet some towels, and sloshed out the scattered fires.

The assault did procure one redeeming effect: the next night, as I ladled melted beeswax onto my dwarfed foot, I had occasion to stare at my hands, and I rediscovered the tiny scratch the apothecary had left on my palm during our minute transaction. While waiting for my new appendage to solidify, I fit my fingernail into the fine groove and slid it back and forth, amplifying the line.

Ignoring them became simple when they reached squirrel proportions, excepting the few times I had to disengage a coil spring trap they'd set at the bottom of the stairs, and once under the welcome mat outside the door. They didn't know it, but I liked guessing where the trap would appear next, and even made bets with myself on the back of the pharmacist's receipt, which I rolled into a scroll and kept in a chink between two log beams. After the trap became too heavy, I found them lurking together behind the toilet wielding corn-on-the-cob skewers, and I snatched them up, threw them into a garbage sack, and carried them down to the water. When I got there, I ran in up past my knees and then quit, with bag in one hand and skewer in the other, to stare at a duck floating on the inanimate water under the dock, while the mallard she hid from skimmed back and forth a few paces off, squawking for her. Without much ado I went back to shore and let them go. The duck stared at me with silver eyes while they scurried up the granite slabs we used for stepping stones and let themselves in through the cat flap.

Finally the day came for journeying into town. I scoured everywhere for them, in all the usual places, behind the fire grate, on the bathmat, aboard a dust ball I'd left in the corner of their bedroom so they would have somewhere to sleep. Eventually I gave up the search and hobbled off on my own. I had nothing to trade except some raspberry tarts. The cub paw I kept for luck.

MICHELE SERWATUK

MY EYES ARE DIM

Sister Eavan kneels down and scrabbles through webs of dirt, looking for her new eyeglasses. There is no diesel for the generator and the batteries in her flashlight are dead, so she places a spluttering candle on the ground. She gropes around in the dark, sifting through clumps of sand and splayed concrete, and finds them lodged in the shattered roots of a calabash tree. In the muted light of the candle, the lenses appear scraped and the right frame is bent, but they are intact. She brushes the filth and debris from them with her fingertips, puts them on, and pushes herself into a standing position.

The last time that she needed new glasses was years ago. She remembers sitting in the common room with René and Antoine. They were watching the new television that Father Dalcour had bought for the school. Unsure of what was happening on the screen, she thought that she saw the bald Irish singer, the O'Connor girl, who came from the same Dublin neighbourhood as she did, ripping up a picture of the Pope. She adjusted and readjusted her lenses, and yes, the Holy

Father, John Paul II, had indeed been dissected. René threw her a sideways glance, trying to gauge her response, but she simply took off her glasses, wiped them, popped them back on the bridge of her nose, and kept her views to herself. Now, with this new prescription, she sees the birthmark on Father Dalcour's neck in a much higher resolution than before. *It is true, what they say, that they look like maps. Something topographical, birthmarks and moles*, she thinks. *This one looks like County Fermanagh.*

"Sister, are you listening?" he asks. "It has been three days and most of the children are asleep. We must either find a way to bury them or pull them out."

At first, the blood was a blinding crimson, like a matador's cape, and gave off a strong metallic scent. Now, as it has pooled in the ruts of the soil and turned a rich russet colour, it reeks like the cancer of someone rotting from the core.

Sister Tallie had offered to go back into the classroom for Eavan's guitar during the picnic. Serafine followed to round up the rest of the students. About twenty of the younger children, who were giggling and quite fidgety in anticipation of the singalong, had already assembled in the courtyard. She had asked them to choose a song.

"*La chanson Quartermaster, Evie. Cette chanson,*" Gaétan, a small boy, sitting cross-legged on the lawn shovelling rice and beans into his mouth, announced with conviction. This was the song that Tallie had taught them during her first week at the school, announcing that it would be a fun way for the children to improve their English. Eavan led with the first line, and the children joined in without bothering to wait for musical accompaniment.

There are apes, apes, eating all the grapes
In the store, in the store,
There are apes, apes, eating all the grapes
In the quartermaster's store.

My eyes are dim, I cannot see,
I have not brought my specs with me,
I have not brought my specs with me.

There are beans, beans, big as submarines . . .

There are bees, bees with little knobby knees . . .

The last thing that Eavan heard was Tallie's rosary beads, wrapped around the belt loop of her jeans, clack against the wall as she swung around to open the door. This was followed by a barely audible squeak that escaped from Serafine's lips. The walls trembled and began to crack into strange zigzagged fissures and then heaved inward in a huge tidal wave. The floor buckled under and swallowed them.

"I'm sorry, Father," is all that Eavan can muster. This phrase, *I'm sorry*, appears in her conversation more and more as she tries to navigate her way through the dense fog of death and decay. Sometimes it comes at the beginning of a sentence, sometimes in the middle, and sometimes at the end. Most of the time, though, it just hovers there, suspended, not connected to any other phrase or thought.

Father Dalcour has secured three working flashlights and sets them on a desk that had catapulted into the yard during the last aftershock. He squats down into the gloomy shafts of light and starts to tug. There is resistance, but he continues to yank at Tallie's shoulder, and then moves in closer to grapple with her neck. The usually unflappable priest breaks into a sweat, trying to extricate her upper body from between two slabs of cement, one of which he has resourcefully jimmied up with a tire jack. Eavan does not move. She rubs her sleeve against her lenses and shudders as plumes of dust float away and bring the scene into sharper focus. Tallie's scapula pokes upward through her skin. The lower part of her arm and the side of her face are smashed, comminuted to a fine, white porridge. During the last convulsion, six hours before, the rubble regurgitated the lower part of her body so that her legs stood straight up, as though she was in midcartwheel. With the next quake, they became impaled on a huge shard of stained glass that had flown eastward from the church. Serafine, whose face is now visible, eyes burst open like two black bullet holes, is pinned under Tallie.

They had finished afternoon classes, and Eavan was arranging plates of food on the backyard table for the picnic. Most of the older children were lined up alongside of the confessional waiting for Father Dalcour, who was still in the garden. Antoine, a former student and now the custodian, was applying a fresh coat of lemon oil to the last row of pews. Tallie had just conducted the younger children through a recitation of the Apostle's Creed and shooed them out into the courtyard.

"We usually do the Nicene," Eavan insisted. "It's what I've taught them."

"Well, why would you do that? The Apostle's is shorter." Tallie smiled. "Who doesn't like the occasional short cut?"

Tallie had arrived from a large parish in Boston two months into the school year and made a crash-hot impression on everyone. Everyone but Eavan. She smoked more Gitanes than an over-caffeinated French actress and moved like a whirlwind. She was startlingly clear-eyed, perpetually happy, and consumed with a light, almost diaphanous energy. Father Dalcour found her boundless energy and unconventional approach refreshing, but didn't know what to make of her wardrobe, which consisted of an array of T-shirts with slogans that said things like "Bummer Man," and "The more you complain, the longer God will let you live." That day's selection was an indigo T-shirt with a winking Buddha silk-screened in the centre. It said "Bad Karma."

In her first week, Tallie had won over René, Antoine, and some of the older boys by kicking the soccer ball around with them after supper and allowing them to sponge a few cigarettes. She also rated high with Serafine and her friends after she loaned out her iPod, one that was loaded with American Top Forty songs and some early *mizik rasin*, which was apparently making a comeback. This prompted Serafine to rap something about Eavan being "*too old skool*" to Tallie's "*rock-star cool.*"

At first, Eavan chafed at the simple fact of Tallie's presence and how acutely aware it made her of her own personal shortcomings, namely her inability to connect with the older kids. She and Father Dalcour, both in their mid-fifties and having been at the school for over twenty years, had yet to propel themselves into the technology of the twenty-first century. Tallie arrived armed with gifts, donations of hand-held video games, several new laptops, and a few cell phones rigged with the ringtones of *Jimmy O.* These would often erupt during class and meal time, throwing Eavan into a tailspin and leading her to believe that she had no means to compete with any device designed for a population that now had the attention span of a lightning bolt. Although she baulked at some of Tallie's teaching methods, like her abbreviated versions of daily prayers, her sluggishness in learning Creole, and her barely passable attempts at French, Eavan had to concede to a most important truth. From the moment she arrived, Tallie was a magnet. All of the children were drawn to her.

"Stand tall and let yourself bloom, my little flowers," she would announce at the end of each kindergarten class. Eavan thought that the cheese factor in these little adages was high, but they never failed to inspire. As soon as Tallie delivered them, Eavan could see the smaller boys puffing out in little barrel-chested swaggers and the girls gliding around the room like little swans. Then Tallie would empty her knapsack and ply them all with *dous makós.*

Viens ici, mes petites fleurs became code for *Candy, we are getting more candy from the new teacher.* They would rush her, practically wrestling her to the ground, to get at the blocks of sweets.

The episode lasted less than a minute. It was apocalyptic. The buildings offered no struggle as they violently pancaked inward. During the first jolt, Eavan's glasses were swept off her face and flung beyond the rattling structures. This sudden myopia provided a small pocket of relief for her as objects in the distance became distorted. She could not see the breadth of the destruction or the victims being consumed by it. She was astonished at her own agility and the precision with which she leapt forward from one swatch of rumbling earth to another, scissoring her legs as if she were jumping ice floes. Like a divining rod, she located and snatched three children into her arms at once and stumbled away from the opening recesses. She repeated this scoop-and-run technique until all of the children were safely deposited on what appeared to be the only section of level ground.

When it stopped, the silence was alarming. None of the children she rescued made a sound. There were no cries, no screams. They huddled in the corner of the yard, trembling like a dock of condemned prisoners, their small faces ossified and caked in blood, and their clothes crusted in a thick, grey silt. She plotted her way over to them, crouched down, and began to check for broken bones. Miraculously, all that she discovered were a few cuts and several small wounds.

She heard Father Dalcour yelling her name, but could not see him through the haze of skyscraping dust and debris. She followed his voice through the shadows and stumbled upon him dragging Antoine's body from the entrance of where the apse once stood. They grabbed at several stray linen cloths that had quivered out from the ruins of the sacristy and tried to staunch his wounds. Antoine sputtered like a sprinkler and hovered in and out of consciousness. As Father Dalcour performed the last rites, Antoine bolted upright from the ground into a sitting position, looked directly into Eavan's eyes, and whispered, "*Ne désespérer pas, ma soeur,*" then died.

By nightfall of that first day, the entire perimeter of the property had become an abattoir with body parts wedged between or sticking out from collapsed walls and buttresses, compressed slabs of chalky cement, and shredded wood. Everyone who had been inside of the church, the school, and the orphanage, was dead. Father Dalcour frantically circled the wreckage, draping linens and blankets over the exposed corpses so the surviving children would not have to look at them.

The next morning, as small shafts of sunlight lapped against her face, Eavan woke to the sound of stuttering gunshots coming from the streets. She realized that she had fallen asleep standing against the back of an overturned school bus. She rubbed her eyes with the heels of her palms and remembered that her glasses were still missing. She considered this a small blessing as it prevented her from absorbing the scope of the detritus surrounding her. Father Dalcour, who she was certain had not slept at all, was sidling toward her through the carpets of debris, his vestments smothered in mud and dirt.

"I have taken inventory," he declared, almost pleased with himself. "Eight towels, six bed sheets, and three blankets. Two broken pews. A couple of strips of tarpaulin from the garden shed, and enough food and water from the picnic to last us for several days." He also confirmed that there was no access to the town so neither of them would be able to leave and look for help. The road in front of the church had collapsed into three large chasms that were too unstable to be traversed.

With unwavering discipline, she and Father Dalcour work into the night, successfully unearthing Tallie and Serafine. They will be buried beside Antoine. After placing both bodies on a couple of makeshift litters they had crafted from an unhinged door and a broken pew, Eavan begins to pray.

"God our Father, Your power brings us to birth, Your providence guides our lives, and by Your command we return to dust."

She cannot continue as a fresh swell of pain resurfaces. Her glasses are so veiled with tears that she does not see Father Dalcour standing beside her.

"I know it feels that we have been forgotten, but God is always with us." He cups her chin in a small pat of affection, then turns away to embark on some greater crusade.

Eavan weeps for a few moments, then takes a deep breath and collects herself as a small aftershock disturbs the ground momentarily. One of the flashlights, sitting on the desk, begins to flicker over the sleeping children. She looks down on Gaétan, sleeping soundly, strangely unaffected and not crippled by grief. She cleans off her glasses, places them on her nose, and settles down to watch the thready little pulse flutter in his neck.

MICHELLE WINTERS

TOUPÉE

I saw him on the subway for the first time the day I brought the meat bomb to work. He wore the most glorious toupée. It was the colour of a fox with the front curled under in a Prince Valiant thing that continued on around the sides and back of his head. It didn't blend in whatsoever with the rest of his real hair, which was a wispy greyish brown. The toupée had a side part that didn't so much part the hair as simply create a break in the bangs to indicate where a real part would be. The hair itself was just like a helmet or a cushion molded to his head.

We were on the same packed car and I had to stand on my toes to reach the hand strap, which gave me a better view down the train. I saw him appear when a man and a woman standing close together moved their heads to opposite edges of my field of vision, just enough to reveal him. He was reading the paper and looked genuinely happy. He was actually smiling. He didn't look crazy or simple, only like he was having a nice time finding out the news. He wore a dark green suit from an indefinable era.

You could tell that as a young man he had been extremely handsome. Like a film star. Even though he wasn't looking up from his paper, it was clear that he knew he was being watched. A man as handsome as he would once have been is always aware of being watched. He had all the confidence of a man with a head of lush, flowing hair all his own.

As his eyes reached the bottom of the paper and he was shaking it out to turn the page, he looked right up, directly at me, and winked.

The doors opened at my stop and I shuffled out with everybody else, looking back to see if he was still there. He wasn't.

Nobody winks at me. People rarely look at me. Obviously, he knew about the bomb. I almost backed out of the whole thing then and there.

But then I thought about Glenn.

When I got to work that morning, I planted the bomb in the hole behind the stereo cabinet. Then I put on a pot of coffee and started peeling eight pounds of potatoes to stick in a bucket of cold water for the day. Glenn wouldn't be in for another half hour, so I didn't even have to sneak around. I have opened up the restaurant every morning for the past four years. To peel potatoes.

Working with Glenn makes me want to set things on fire. I hate him for employing me, I hate him for being who he is, and I hate him for imposing his flaccid proximity on me. But when I think of leaving, I don't see another job, another boss, another life. I see only his pasty face. And it makes me hate him more.

I had found the hole in the cabinet a few weeks earlier when I was dusting. It looked like someone had kicked it or possibly termites had eaten through it. It was jagged and in a spot down by the baseboard that was impossible for Glenn to see, because it would require bending over, and he's a million years old with a bad back. If he has to reach his fingertips further down than his knees to get something, he asks someone to get it for him. He should really be in a nursing home, or a museum, but as the *owner* he feels he has to be present at the restaurant as an ambassador to the clientele, who can't stand him. Whenever he musters up the generosity to send a very weak drink to the table of some important patron and minces over to shake their hand, trying to look magnanimous, you can see the mild distaste forming on their faces as he approaches. Then his weedy handshake seals their revulsion. You don't need to know Glenn to hate him; you only have to see him.

I had been thinking about the bomb for a while, but when I found the hole in the stereo case, I figured it must be a sign.

The thing about the stereo is that Glenn worked in *radio* forty years ago and feels he still has his finger on the pulse of what's hip and hot with the kids. He programs the music for the evening in the restaurant, then locks up the stereo in the cupboard and takes home the key. Even though he knows we can't get at the stereo and have to languish for the entire shift, listening to instrumental covers of the Beach Boys, he still calls in the middle of the night and demands that we hold the phone up to the speakers so he can hear for sure that the rotation hasn't been tampered with. Everybody hates the music there. Everybody has complained to him about it and he smiles his insipid smile, nods calmly, and says, "Well, I'll look into that." He'll never look into that.

—

The next week on my way to work, I saw the man again. This time he wasn't reading anything; he was just sitting with his hands folded in his lap.

I was standing facing the doors, and since he was sitting sideways in his seat, he was staring right at my back. As I looked at my own reflection in the darkened window of the train, I noticed him behind me, also looking at my reflection.

He saw me see him.

I unintentionally raised my eyebrows.

He intentionally raised his eyebrows back.

I averted my gaze because the last thing I wanted to do was play the mirror game with a psycho on the subway, only to have him follow me to work and be sitting outside at the end of the night, ready to follow me home. This would invariably be the thing that would happen.

I unfocused my eyes to avoid his gaze and as I did, in my peripheral vision, I saw his hand slowly move up toward his face and touch the edge of his rug at me like a cowboy tipping his hat.

I couldn't think of how to respond. He saw me see him again, so I nodded, just barely, in return. Then he shook his head sternly at me and smiled almost paternally, as though I had done something that wasn't really bad, and he kind of approved in a way, but he trusted that I would take care of it because I knew right from wrong. Then he nodded to himself, folding his arms and resting his chin on his chest.

He didn't look up for the rest of the ride.

When I got to work I took the bomb out of its hiding place and had a good look at it. It seemed to be working. There was an active white foam bubbling all around the chicken gizzards and guts. The meat was fermenting in milk. The pressure would overpower the glass of the jar and it would blow within a couple of weeks. The smell would be unbearable. Glenn would have to replace that wall and possibly the entire floor. He might have to abandon the restaurant, or it might have to be torn down. More than anything though, he would run around just furious, screaming like a preschooler, veins bulging through the papery, translucent skin on his temples. He might even have a heart attack. I held onto the jar for a minute, transported. Glenn would be wearing shorts, beige shorts with black socks and black shoes, as he did in the summer. I could hear the pitch of his squeal when he demanded to know who could possibly have done such a thing.

I put the bomb back in its hiding place.

Glenn has a trick he does that he thinks is really good. He finds a cigarette butt outside and picks it up, presumably with a stick with a nail through it or a really long pair of tweezers, and he puts it on the steps out front and waits to see how long it takes one of the staff members to see it and pick it up. Then he comes into the kitchen and announces how many days it's been there with no one noticing. Glenn believes in the kind of employee loyalty that would make someone stop and pick up a cigarette butt on the stairs because it was marring the beauty of their place of work.

"You'd pick it up if this was your own house, wouldn't you?" he whines. "Why can't you keep my restaurant clean? Is it disdain? You can tell me."

He keeps up the cigarette trick and we all play along now, which isn't hard because the cigarette butt is always in the same place. We try to pick it up the second he puts it there, which makes it like a game. The whole point of his trick, Glenn doesn't realize, is defeated now, because our picking up the cigarette butt doesn't mean anyone cares any more about the well-being of the restaurant, but it certainly does make him feel as though his stupid crybaby will is being obeyed, which is more important to him than even employee loyalty.

I had started dreaming about the bomb every night, and was getting downright giddy every time I looked at Glenn, which I had to try to conceal because smiling at him would have been so out of character as to give me away.

I hadn't seen the man on the subway for a couple of weeks and had started to feel that I was in the clear.

Then this happened:

I was on my way to work, as usual, when I saw him. He was a few yards away, near the end of the car. He wasn't sitting, even though there were seats available. He was standing next to the pole, but he wasn't holding on to it. He looked bad. I had to really squint to make sure it was him, but his rug was unmistakable. Just as I was looking, not sure what to do, the front of his toupée stood up from his head, just lifted right up. He didn't seem to notice. The rug stayed that way, looking at me for a second. Then it addressed me.

"He's sick," it said.

It didn't have eyes or fangs or anything; it was just standing up, talking. It had a soft, deep voice.

"If you let this happen," it told me, "it will kill him." I was frozen on the spot, staring back at the rug, which, even though it didn't have eyes, was giving me a very serious look. We stood like this for the rest of the ride. When the doors opened at my stop, I nodded slightly and then the rug nodded back, flopping up once and coming down to rest on the man's head.

I would get rid of the bomb. I would throw it in the river.

I walked as fast as I could to work and was almost running when I rounded the comer and the smell stopped me like a wall. It very nearly knocked me down. It was how you might imagine the smell of an open mass grave. Next to a latrine. I doubled over and gagged a few times with my hands on my knees. Then I looked down the street at the restaurant and saw Glenn on the steps.

He was sitting there with his head in his hands. He wasn't screaming or scampering around like a gerbil; he was just sitting, looking at the ground.

With my nose buried in my arm, I made my way over. He looked up when he saw my feet in front of him, and I saw it in his eyes: the pain of a full grown child still getting his lunch money stolen every single day in the schoolyard. Glenn lied to himself a lot, but as much as he wanted to believe that as a successful restaurateur and former radio celebrity he was loved and respected by his clientele and staff, he knew that people simply didn't like him. He knew that people made fun of him. He had heard them in the kitchen.

"What is it, Janine?" he asked. He really wanted to know. "Is it – is it disdain? Is it . . ." He shook his head and trailed off as his voice filled with tears.

I sat down on the steps beside him and hesitated a second before putting my arm around his frail little shoulders. This made him start crying harder. I felt something let go inside of me, put my other arm around him, and pulled him close. I actually squeezed him. This made him start sobbing so hard he felt like he was breaking apart, so I squeezed him tighter, hoping my arms might hold the pieces of him together.

D.W. WILSON

THE DEAD ROADS

One time we roadtripped across the country with Animal Brooks, and he almost got run over by a pickup truck partway through Alberta. It was me and my twenty-year-old girlfriend Vic and him, him in his cadpat jumpsuit, Vic in her flannel logger coat and her neon hair that glowed like a bush lamp. We'd known Animal since grade school: the north-born shit kicker, like Mick Dundee. A lone ranger, or something. Then in 2002 the three of us crammed into his '67 Camaro to tear-ass down the Trans-Canada at eighty miles an hour. Vic and me had a couple hundred bucks and time to kill before she went back to university. That'd make it August, or just so. Animal had a way of not caring too much and a way of hitting on Vic. He was twenty-six and hunted-looking, with engine-grease stubble and red eyes sunk past his cheekbones. In his commie hat and Converses he had that hurting lurch, like a scrapper's swag, dragging foot after foot with his knees loose and his shoulders slumped. He'd drink a garden hose under the table if it looked at him wrong. He once boned a girl in some poison ivy bushes, but was a gentleman about it. An ugly dent caved his forehead, and rumours around Invermere said he'd been booted by a cow and then survived.

Vic stole shotgun right from the get-go and Animal preferred a girl beside him, anyway, so I squished in the back among our gear. We had a ton of liquor but only a two-man tent because Animal didn't care one way or the other. He'd packed nothing but his wallet and a bottle-rimmed copy of *The Once and Future King*, and he threatened to beat me to death with the Camaro's dipstick if he caught me touching his book. His brother used to read it to him before bed, and that made it an item of certain value, a real point of civic pride.

The Camaro's vinyl seats smelled like citrus cleaner. First time I ever got a girl pregnant was in Animal's backseat, but I didn't want to mention it since Vic would've ditched out then and there. Vic'll crack you with a highball glass if you say the wrong thing, she can do that. We weren't really dating, either. She just came home in the summers to visit her old man and score a few bucks slopping mortar, and we'd hook up. I don't know anyone prettier than Vic. She's got a heart-shaped face and sun freckles on her chin and a lazy eye when she drinks and these wineglass-sized breasts I get to look at sometimes. On the West Coast she bops around with a university kid who wears a sweater and carries a man purse. Her dad showed me a picture of the guy, all milk jug ears and a pinched nose that'd bust easy in a fight. Upper-middle-class, horizon-in-his-irons, that type. Not that I can really complain, I guess. Vic never mentioned him and I never mentioned him and we went about our business like we used to, like when we were sixteen and bent together in the old fur trading fort up the beach on Kopokol Road.

Vic planned our journey with a 1980s road atlas she snagged from her dad's material shed. Animal kept his hand on the stick shift so he could zag around lorries hauling B.C. timber to the tar sands. Whenever he geared to fifth his palm plopped onto Vic's thigh. Each time, she'd swat him and give him the eyebrow, and he'd wink at me in the rear-view. —Dun worry Duncan, I wouldn't do that tuh ya, he'd say, but I know Animal.

For the first day we plowed east through the national park. Cops don't patrol there so Animal went batshit. His Camaro handled like a motor bike and it packed enough horse to climb a hill in fifth, and I don't know if he let off the gun the whole way. He held a Kokanee between his legs and gulped it whenever the road straightened. Animal was a top-notch driver. As a job, he manned a cargo truck for this organic potato delivery service. One time he spun an e-brake slide at forty miles per hour, so me and him could chase down these highschoolers who'd hucked a butternut squash through his windshield.

To kill time, Animal bought a *Playboy* and handed it to Vic. He suggested she do a dramatic read if possible. At first she gave him the eye, but he threatened to have me do it if not her. He also handed her all the receipts for gas and food and booze to keep track of, on account of her higher education, but I'm not even sure Vic did much math. At university she studied biology and swamplands, and I like to think I got her into it, since there's a great wide marsh behind this place we used to get shitfaced at. It's a panelboard bungalow on the outskirts of town, built, Vic figures, on floodland from the Columbia River. Vic and me used to stash our weed in the water, pinned under the vegetable band. One time we stole election signs and ditched them in the marsh, and the Valley Echo printed a headline that said the cops didn't know to call it vandalism or a political statement. Neither did I really, since Vic planned the whole thing. Then last summer I asked her to muck around the marsh with me but she said we really shouldn't, because it's drying up. She had a bunch of science to prove it. —Something has to change, Dunc, she said, pawing at me. —Or there'll be nothing left.

Eventually Animal bored of the Trans-Canada, so he veered onto some single lane switchback that traced the Rocky Mountains north. I thought Vic'd be distressed but turned out she expected it. She shoved the road atlas under the seat and dug a baggie of weed from her pack. Later, we played punch buggy, but I couldn't see much from the back, and Vic walloped me on the charley horse so goddamn hard I got gooseskins straight down to my toes.

The sign said, *Tent Camping – $15*, and Animal said, —Fuck that shit, and then he booted the sign pole for good measure. He plunked himself on the Camaro's cobalt hood and rubbed his eyes. We'd been on the road for a while, and I don't remember if he ever slept much. The air smelled like forest fire and it also reeked of cow shit, but Alberta usually reeks like cow shit. Vic leaned into the doorframe, hip cocked to one side like a teenager. Her flannel sleeves hung too low and she bunched the extra fabric in each fist. She chewed a piece of her hair. When we used to date I would tug those strands out of her mouth and she'd ruck her eyebrows to a scowl and I'd scramble away before she belted me one. In the low Albertan dusk her bright hair was the colour of whiskey. She caught me staring, winked.

Vic slid her hands in her jean pockets. —I got fifteen bucks.

—Yah I bet yuh do, Animal said.

—What the hell does that mean?

—Et's Duncan's cash ennet?

—Just some, Vic said.

—I got more money en Duncan, yuh know.

—Shut your mouth Animal, I told him.

—Jus sayen, he said, and ducked into driver's.

We reached some place called Shellyoak and Animal called all eyes on the lookout for a campsite. He drove through the town's main haul, where the Camaro's wide nose spanned the lane past centre. A ways out, the Rockies marked the border home. This far north their surfaces were dotted with pine husks – grey, chewed-out shells left over from the pine beetle plague. Not a living tree in sight. Shellyoak's buildings were slate brick with round chimneys and tiny windows high as a man's chin. A group of kids smoked dope on a street bench and Vic hollered for directions and one waved up the lane with an arm so skinny it flailed like an elastic. —Near the amusement park, he called.

Big rocks broke the landscape on Shellyoak's outskirts, and Vic figured it used to be under a glacier. Animal was dead silent the whole way. I guess the bony trees irked him, that carcass forest. The stink of wood smoke blasted from the radiator and it reminded me of the chimneys that burned when I used to scrape frost off Vic's windshield, all those mornings after I stayed the night at her place. Her dad would be in the kitchen as I tried to sneak out, and he'd hand me a coffee and the ice shears and tell me to keep in his good books. One time he said Vic and me made a good pair, us two, but if I got her pregnant he'd probably beat me to death with an extension cord. He grinned like a boy, I remember. Then he said, —Seriously though, ya make a good pair. A few minutes later, Vic tiptoed downstairs and her old man clapped me on the shoulder like a son, and Vic smiled as if she could be happier than ever.

Animal yawed us around a bend and all at once the horizon lit up with a neon clown head big as an RV. From our angle, it looked as if the clown also had rabbit ears, flopped down like two bendy fluorescent scoops. The highway'd gone gravel and the Camaro's tires pinged pebbles on the undercarriage. In the distance I saw a ferris wheel rocking like a treetop, but not much else in the park to speak of. Animal geared down and this time when he laid his palm on Vic's knee he didn't take it off, and she didn't smack him. He still winked at me in the rear-view, though.

—Christ, it's a gas station too, Vic said, pointing at the pumps hidden in the clown's shadow. Animal steered toward them, tapped the fuel gauge with its needle at quarter-tank.

—You got enough, I said, but he didn't so much as grunt.

He parked at the first pump and unfolded from the vehicle. Vic popped her seat forward so I could climb out. Figures milled inside the gas station and their outlines peered through the glass. A painted sign that said *Tickets 5 bucks* hung above the door. On it, somebody'd drawn a moose.

Animal started pumping gas. He tweaked his eyebrows at me. —Well?

—The hell do you want now, I said.

—Go enside and ask where we cen camp, he said. He winked over my shoulder, at Vic. —Giddyup now.

—They'll tell us to go to the pay grounds.

—Kid said we cen camp near the amusement park.

—That kid was on dope, I said.

—Yer on dope, he shot, and thrumped his fingers on the Camaro's hood. He flashed his gums. —Go on, skinny.

—What the fuck, Animal.

—Yer in muh way, skinny, he said, and cocked his head to indicate Vic. —I seen better windows en you.

Then the station's storm door clattered and Vic yelped and I turned and saw the biggest goddamn Native man ever. He wore Carhartts and steel-toes and no shirt beneath the straps. The buckles dimpled his collar. His hair gummied to his cheeks and his head tilted at an angle. This gruesome, spider-like scar spanned his chest and the whole left nipple was sliced off, snubbed like a button nose. He leaned an arm-length calliper on his neck. Then his face jerked into a smile, but not a friendly kind. —I never seen a Camaro can run on diesel, he said, stressing his *e*'s.

For a second he stood there in the doorway as if he might say *gotcha!* Vic bunched excess sleeve in her fists and I sniffed the air to see if the place reeked like diesel engines, the smell of carbide and tar and dirty steel. Animal stared straight at the Native guy, as if in a game of chicken instead of wrecking his engine with the wrong fuel, as if he just needed to overcome something besides the way things actually were, as if he could just *be* stubborn enough. Then he killed the pump and yanked the nozzle from his tank. —Where the fuck's et say?

The guy did a shrug-a-lug. —It's a trucker stop.

—Yah well I'm not uh trucker.

—Me neither, the guy said, and moved between Vic and me, toward the car, and the air that wafted after him stunk of B.O.

His neck muscles strained to hold his head straight, like he was used to keeping it down. A scrapper's stance, almost. I caught Vic's attention and her forehead scrunched up and the skin at her eyes tightened like old leather. I'd never known her to be the worrying type.

—Nice car though, the guy said. He dragged a wide hand over the Camaro's cobalt finish.

—Yah et is.

—I'm Walla, he said, and swung his head to Vic. —This your girlfriend?

Animal banged his commie hat against his knuckles. —Ya got uh pump er somthen?

—Nup, Walla said, and stressed the *p*.

—Or somthen else?

—Buddy has a siphon.

—Can we get et?

—Nup. Tomorrow, I bet.

Animal's mouth jawed in circles and I could all but hear his brain trying to find a way to make it all go right.

—There a campsite nearby? I said, to buy time.

Walla twitched his head behind him. —The summit. Not like she's a real mountain, though. You owe me $12.37 for the diesel.

—The hells I do, Animal said, and crossed his arms.

Walla set the callipers on the Camaro's hood and their measurement end tinked. He swung his gaze from me to Animal to Vic, then to Animal, and then at the shop. He stood nearest Vic of all, a full two-and-a-half heads taller than her, and I swear to God he had hands big as mudflaps. —No, he said, very slowly, —you do.

Vic dug cash from her wallet, fifteen bucks. She handed it over and Walla tugged the bills one at a time. —I'll get your change, he said, and stepped toward the station. Then, over his shoulder: —You can't leave your car there. He grinned at Vic and his teeth were white as gold. —Well, maybe you cen. Push her outta the way of the pump.

I got behind the Camaro. Animal hung at the gas tank like one of those old guys who hope somebody'll come talk to them. —Put her in neutral, idiot, I snapped, and dug my toes into the ground and heaved and the Camaro rocked. Vic pressed her back to the bumper. —What's happening, she whispered to me, but I grunted and got the car rolling.

We pushed the Camaro outside the clown face's shadow and I put myself between Vic and the station. Walla reappeared, horselike in his gait. He dumped the coins in my palm and ran his tongue over his teeth. He touched a notch under his jaw. —The summit'd be a helluva climb, he said. —Especially if you're taking your booze. I got a pickup.

—We can hike it, I said.

—Trade you a lift.

—Fer what, Animal barked.

—What ya got? Walla said, and rubbed his triceps. The scar-tissue on his chest looked sun-dried, pinker than it ought to, and in the sticky neon light it shone raw and oily like a beating. —Aw hell, he said, —I'll help you out. Get yer stuff.

We grabbed our beer cooler and Vic took the sleeping bag and Animal pocketed *The Once and Future King*. Walla disappeared around the gas station and a few minutes later he came chewing up gravel in a green three-seater Dodge. He was sardined in driver's with his shoulders hunched and his knees against his armpits. The truck had a bust-out rear window and poly duct-taped in the gap. Horse quilts blanketed the box, warm with the smell of dog.

—One of you needs to sit in the bed, Walla said, then dangled his keys, —and one of you needs to drive, cause I'm shittered, and the fucking pigs have it out for me.

Animal lunged for the keys and me and him shared this moment between us, his mouth twisted like a grin, and I wanted to hit him so bad. But if I wailed on him I'd look bad to Vic, so I climbed into the mess of bedding while Animal drove the switchback. The truck whipped around bends and I imagined Walla's skunky B.O. sneaking through the patched-up window, how bad it must've been in the cab with him. Animal was goddamn lucky he'd pocketed his book. The whole way, Vic shifted uncomfortably, and I could hear her thighs brushing Walla on one side and Animal on the other.

Atop the summit, Walla showed us a fire pit ringed by skeleton trees where he'd piled some chopped wood. Animal collapsed near the pit to work a blaze. He waved Vic off when she offered to help, so she dug a mickey of Canadian Club from the cooler. Fifty feet off, a cliff-side dropped to the highway below, where the ferris wheel keeled and the goddamn clown face smirked.

—Thanks for helping us, Vic said. She sat down on an upturned log, whiskey on her knee.

—My dad tells me if you're cooking stew, and you don't put meat in it, you can't bitch when yer eating it, Walla said, and he grinned to show his pearly teeth, and Vic laughed and so did I, though I didn't know what the hell he meant. Then he said:

—Now I need a lift down to the station.

Vic froze in the middle of sipping her whiskey and Animal looked up from his smouldering fire. —What'dya mean.

—I told you, I'm shittered, and the pigs have it out for me.

—I'm buildin' the fire, Animal said, but Walla had his eyes on Vic, anyway. Vic glanced from Walla to me and I knew she wouldn't ask me to step in, because she won't do that, ever. One time she figured out how to fix a circuit fault on her Ranger all her own, because she didn't want to ask her old man how.

—I'll do it, I said to Walla, and then I dumped my half-empty beer over Animal's wimpy fire and he cursed at me like a foreman.

Walla flicked me his keys and I palmed them from the air and got in the driver seat, and he swung into passenger like a buddy. Not thirty seconds into the drive his stench soured up the cab, but at least he smelled like a working man, like he just forgot to shower, and not like some hobo. On the way down, the poly over the rear panel smacked about and more than once he leaned sideways to inspect the tape. He spread one leg across the seat, draped his arm clear out the window, and I half-wondered if his knuckles bobbed along the gravel. In the distance, the horizon glowed from the park lights and the treetops resembled hundreds of heated needles. I kept the high beams on and scanned for marble eyes, but Walla told me the all the deer fled north with the beetles. —Nothin' here but us and the flies, he said. —Gas, bloodweed. A thousand dead acres.

—The dead roads, or something.

—I don't mind that, Walla said. Then: —They're an odd couple, eh?

—Who.

—The girl and him, Animal.

—They're not a couple.

—Sure they are. Or gonna be, he said, and punched me on the arm like we were friends. —The way he looks at her? Sure.

—He looks at all girls like that. Walla smiled like a mason jar. He had fillings in his teeth. —Her, too. She was lookin' at him too.

The station and the clown face swept into view and I geared down and my fist touched Walla's knee and I imagined Vic and Animal bent together at his shitty fire, red marks scraped over Vic's neck and collarbones from his barbed-wire stubble.

—You got a thing for her eh, he said.

—No.

—Might be you need to take him down a notch.

—We're buds, I said, and parked the truck.

Walla extracted himself from the passenger seat. —Nah man, he said across the hood, *—we're* buds.

Whatever the hell he meant I'll never know, since I ditched him and started walking back along the road, toward the summit. The whole way I thought about Animal and Vic and I tried not think about them at the same time. I'd known them so long. The outside smelled more like driftwood than a forest. Wind kicked dirt at my face, and though it breezed around the treetops they just creaked like power poles. I wouldn't have been surprised if a goddamn wolfman came pounding out the dark or something. A few times headlights tear-assed up the road and a few times I almost barreled sideways and I just got madder even thinking of it.

Then the slope evened out, which meant I was nearing the summit, and then the trees flickered campfire-orange a short ways off. The road looped our campsite so I cut through the forest. Never been so scared in my life, those last steps. Animal atop Vic, grinding away, probably still in his stupid commie hat and his Converses – no sight in the world could be worse. I'd rather get shot. Walla was right – Animal'd been gunning for her the whole goddamn trip. Right from the start when he kicked me to the backseat, some big plan – some big, selfish plan.

I got close enough to see the flames. Vic sat under her sleeping bag, off near the cliff-side, but I could only make out her outline in the orange light. Animal was MIA. They might have already finished, how could I know. I crept along the tree line, scanned for him. Not sure what I hoped to accomplish. It's not like he kept a dark secret.

I found Animal outside the campsite with his back to the slope and his cock in his hand. It was dark enough that I didn't get the whole picture, thank God for that. He'd crossed the road so he could piss on a big pine that might have been a little bit alive – for some reason he got real uncomfortable around those dead trees. I had some things to say to him. Vic's old man once told me a guy needs to know when to pick his battles, and as I watched Animal, pissing as if nothing mattered, I figured it out: a guy needs to know what he cares about most, and Animal, well, he didn't care about stuff. But he had to know I did. Christ, everybody in the valley knew I did. It'd be like if I tried to steal his car for a joyride. I'm his friend, for fucker's sake.

Then a truck hauled ass up the road, kicking gravel at its mudflaps. It had a good clip and its rear end fishtailed side to side, out of control or so the passengers could get a laugh. Its headlamps swung around but on that switchback the dead trees broke the light – no way the driver would see Animal, not before clobbering him. Animal turned as if to check what the commotion was about. Either he couldn't see or he was too stupid to dive for cover or he figured no truck would dare to run him down. I saw the trajectory, though, loud and clear: the pickup's rear end would swing into him, knock him ass-over-tea-kettle into the woods, and that'd be that for Animal Brooks. But I didn't yell out. I didn't make a sound. Because all I could think of was his hand on Vic's thigh, over and over the whole trip, his wild grin in the rearview, and all the stuff he'd pulled to be alone with her. So nope, I didn't yell out, and the truck fishtailed right toward him and he yowled like a dog and I lost track of where he went.

Vic bolted from the tree line, almost right into me, and I scrambled after her. She gave me a look, as if surprised, but I just nodded like I ought to be there. Animal was already on his feet. Moss and dead twigs stuck to his face and his commie hat had been biffed away and the forest floor was beat up where he'd rolled across it. He pulled a pinecone from his hair and stared at it in wonder.

—Animal, Vic barked, —you okay?

He flicked the pinecone aside, seemed to notice us. —Why the hell didn't yuh say sompthen, he said, staring at me.

—What?

—Yuh were across the road. Why didn't yuh yell out or sompthen. Fucken truck nearly killed me.

—I just got here, I told him.

—Yuh just got here eh.

—Yeah, got back right now. Animal swiped his commie hat from the ground. He banged it against his thigh to dust it off. —Just en time to see muh kung fu reflexes, he said, and grinned.

—So you're okay? Vic said.

—Shaken up, yeah.

Vic grabbed Animal's chin and turned his head sideways. His cheek was scraped and dirty and Vic licked her thumb to rub it clean. —Mighta pulled uh groin muscle, too, he said when she stepped back, and Vic lasted a full two seconds of his leer before she punched him in the chest hard enough to make him wheeze.

Afterward, by the fire, Animal shook out his adrenaline. —Woulda sucked to run that truck over, he said, and laughed – a deep, throaty laugh like a guy does when he's survived an event that should have killed him. Then he dug into the cooler and started skulling beers to drown his jitters.

Vic and me shared a mickey of Canadian Club, away from the campfire so we could look over the cliff-side at this bizarre piece of land. She took a big chug from the bottle and handed it over. Vic can drink like a tradesman when times come. The moonlight made her cheeks silver and that lazy eye of hers acted out. She spread her sleeping bag across her legs and I inched my way under it and the vinyl clung to my shins. Vic smelled like a campfire. Vic smelled like citrus shampoo or something. Vic smelled like Vic.

—This an alright place to sleep, she said and wiggled in the dirt and the dried bloodweed and made a little nest.

—I'm not picky, I said.

—You smell like a dog.

—Sorry, Vic.

She belted me on the shoulder and I leaned into her. Below us, a couple semis zoomed north and the ferris wheel spun and

I thought I could hear Walla chopping lumber. Christ, a weirder place. By the fire, Animal sounded out words from his book, finger under each sentence. Then Vic unbuttoned her flannel coat. She always wore it, or if not the coat then a flannel shirt. Sexiest thing, swear to God. I remember how she took it off, first time we ever boned, all awkward and struggling so I had to help her with the sleeves. A different kind of time back then. A different way of going about things, even. Sometimes I wish I was smarter so I could've gone to university with Vic.

Vic put her hand under my chin and jacked my head to eye level. I guess I was looking at her breasts. She leaned in and kissed me and she tasted all cabbagey like dope, and soft, and her smooth chin ground on my middle-of-the-night stubble. But I couldn't kiss her right then. I don't know why. She slicked her tongue over my lips and I couldn't get my head around the whole thing, the ferris wheel and what Walla said and how I almost got Animal killed, and Vic, you know, and the whole goddamn thing.

—Don't fuck around, she said, but the words were all breath.

—Just thinken is all.

She bit down on my lip. —Well, stop it.

—I like you a lot, Vic.

For a second she stopped and turned her head and her neon hair grazed my nose, and I'd have given anything to know what she was going on in her head right then. She had her lips squished shut and her forehead a little scrunched as if figuring something out – same look as the day she left for university. That'd have been in '99, and her and her old man and me stayed at a hotel in Calgary, so she could catch her west-coast flight in the wee hours, and while she showered her old man told me not to let her get away. —It'll happen Duncan, he said, his face drawn in and lined around his eyes, as if he knew what the hell he was talking about. —I swear to God you'll lose her if you don't take action soon. And I nodded and tried not to grin, because I understood exactly what he meant.

On the mountaintop, Vic hooked hair behind her ear. —You're my guy, Dunc, she said as though it were true.

—I know Vic. But sometimes I don't know. You know?

Then she cuffed me, all playful, and pulled me into her.

But that's Vic for you. Afterward, when we were done and Animal's moans were snores and the fire glowed down to embers, Vic sat up and stretched. Her ribs made bumps under her skin and the muscles along her spine tensed and eased and it felt alright right then. That's Vic for you, that's how she can make you feel, that easy. Never liked a girl so much. Nothing else to it. I just cared about her more than the university guy did or Animal did or maybe her old man did. I should've told her so, or how I wished she didn't have to go west, or how I'd had a ring for her for years but lacked the balls to do anything with it. Even then, the mountaintop seemed like a last chance or something.

She sucked the rest of the whiskey and pointed at the sky where a trail of turquoise streaked across the horizon – the northern lights, earlier than I'd ever known them. She just stood there for a second with her back to me and those lights around her. Christ, she was so pretty. Then she whipped the empty bottle off the summit, and I stared at her and thought about her and waited for the sound of the bottle breaking way, way below us.

ABOUT THE AUTHORS

Jay Brown recently moved to Toronto from Victoria, British Columbia. His award-winning writing has appeared in many journals and magazines across Canada, including *Vancouver Review*, *Prairie Fire*, *Grain*, and, most recently, the anthology *Darwin's Bastards*. He has just completed a fiction collection tentatively titled *The Hollow Earth*. He is at work on more stories and a novel.

Michael Christie received his MFA in Creative Writing from UBC in 2008. Before that, he worked in a homeless shelter in Vancouver's Downtown Eastside and also did outreach helping the severely mentally ill attend court. "The Extra" appears in his fiction collection, *The Beggar's Garden* (HarperCollins Canada, 2011). Another story from this collection, "Goodbye Porkpie Hat," appeared in *The Journey Prize Stories 20*. He lives in Thunder Bay, where he is at work on a novel.

Seyward Goodhand's short fiction has appeared in *Queen Street Quarterly*, *echolocation*, and *PRISM international*. This year, she won a fellowship in the SLS Fiction Poetry Contest. She is currently working on a collection of stories and finishing a doctorate in Early Modern Literature from the University of Toronto.

Miranda Hill is a recent graduate of UBC's Optional Residency MFA program. "Petitions to Saint Chronic" was her first published story. Her fiction has subsequently appeared in *The New Quarterly*, and her collection of stories is forthcoming from Doubleday Canada. Hill is also the founder of Project Bookmark Canada, a national charitable organization that places text from stories and poems in the exact physical locations where literary scenes are set. She lives in Hamilton, Ontario.

Fran Kimmel's short fiction has appeared in *Grain*, *Prairie Fire*, *The Fiddlehead*, *filling Station*, *Room*, *FreeFall Magazine*, and *The Journey Prize Stories 21*. Her writing has been nominated for the CBC Literary Awards, and has won both CBC Anthology and Write for Radio Awards. Born in Calgary, she now lives in Lacombe, Alberta. Her first novel, *The Shore Girl Clippings*, will be published in 2012 by NeWest Press.

Ross Klatte, born in Minneapolis and raised on a Minnesota dairy farm, immigrated to Canada in 1971. His fiction has appeared in *Event* and *The New Orphic Review*, and he is the author of *Leaving the Farm* (Oolichan Books, 2007), a memoir that began as the prize-winning essay for the 1990 CBC Literary Awards. He's now at work on a novel about going back-to-the-land in British Columbia at the end of the Sixties. He and his wife live near Balfour, B.C.

Michele Serwatuk's short fiction and poetry have appeared in *The Antigonish Review*, *Dandelion*, *Grain*, *The New Quarterly*, *Room*, *The Wascana Review*, and other journals. She is a past recipient of the Okanagan Short Story Award. She lives in Toronto where she runs a small animal care business, and is currently working on a non-fiction book entitled *It's Just Us*, on the Canada's public health care system.

Jessica Westhead is a Toronto writer and editor. Her fiction has appeared in a number of literary magazines, including *Geist*, *The New Quarterly*, *Taddle Creek*, *The Puritan*, *The Antigonish Review*, and *Indiana Review*. She was shortlisted for the 2009 CBC Literary Awards, and her first novel, *Pulpy & Midge* (Coach House Books, 2007), was nominated for the ReLit Award. "What I Would Say" was first published by *This Magazine* and appears in her short story collection, *And Also Sharks*, published by Cormorant Books in spring 2011.

D. W. Wilson's short stories and essays have appeared in literary journals across Canada, Ireland, and the United Kingdom. His first book, *Once You Break a Knuckle* – a collection of interconnected short stories set on the west coast – was published by Hamish Hamilton Canada in September 2011. He is a Canadian citizen by birth and temperament, but currently lives in the United Kingdom while he pursues a Ph.D.

Michelle Winters is a translator and technical writer from Saint John, N.B. A founding member of Just in a Bowl Productions, she co-wrote and performed two plays with the company, *Unsinkable* and *The Hungarian Suicide Duel*. Her work has been published in *Peter O'Toole: A Magazine of One-Line Poems* and *This Magazine*. She has just completed a novel entitled *I Am a Truck*, which she hopes people will one day read.

ABOUT THE CONTRIBUTING JOURNALS

For more information about the journals that submitted to this year's competition, The Journey Prize, and *The Journey Prize Stories*, please visit www.mcclelland.com/jps or www.facebook.com/TheJourneyPrize.

The Dalhousie Review has been in operation since 1921 and aspires to be a forum in which seriousness of purpose and playfulness of mind can coexist in meaningful dialogue. The journal publishes new fiction and poetry in every issue and welcomes submissions from authors around the world. Editor: Anthony Stewart. Submissions and correspondence: *The Dalhousie Review*, Dalhousie University, Halifax, Nova Scotia, B3H 4R2. Email: dalhousie.review@dal.ca Website: www.dalhousiereview.dal.ca

The New Orphic Review is a semi-annual literary magazine which publishes fiction and articles up to 10,000 words in length and poetry ranging from sonnets to free verse. It is listed in *Poet's Market, Novel & Short Story Writer's Market, The Pushcart Prize*, and *Best American Short Stories.* It has featured poetry, fiction, and essays by authors from Finland, Switzerland, Italy, Ireland, Britain, Chile, Canada, and the United States. Editor-in-chief: Ernest Hekkanen. Associate Editor: Margrith Schraner. Submissions and correspondence: *The New Orphic Review*, 706 Mill Street, Nelson, British Columbia, V1L 4S5. Website: www3.telus.net/neworphicpublishers-hekkanen

Prairie Fire is a quarterly magazine of contemporary Canadian writing that publishes stories, poems, and literary non-fiction by both emerging and established writers. *Prairie Fire*'s editorial mix also occasionally features critical or personal essays and interviews with authors. Stories published in *Prairie Fire* have won awards at the National Magazine Awards and the Western Magazine Awards. *Prairie Fire* publishes writing from, and has readers in, all parts of Canada. Editor: Andris Taskans. Fiction Editors: Warren Cariou and Heidi Harms. Submissions and correspondence: *Prairie Fire*, Room 423, 100 Arthur Street, Winnipeg, Manitoba, R3B 1H3. Email: prfire@mts.net Website: www.prairiefire.ca

PRISM international, the oldest literary magazine in Western Canada, was established in 1959 by a group of Vancouver writers. Published four times a year, *PRISM* features short fiction, poetry, creative non-fiction, and translations by both new and established writers from Canada and around the world. The only criteria are originality and quality. *PRISM* holds three exemplary competitions: the Short Fiction Contest, the Literary Non-fiction Contest, and the Earle Birney Prize for Poetry. Executive Editors: Elizabeth Hand and Erin Flegg. Fiction Editor: Cara Woodruff. Poetry Editor: Jordan Abel. Submissions and correspondence: *PRISM international*, Creative Writing Program, The University of British Columbia, Buchanan E-462, 1866 Main Mall, Vancouver, British Columbia, V6T 1Z1. Email (for queries only): prism@interchange.ubc.ca Website: www.prismmagazine.ca

Room is Canada's oldest literary journal by and about women. Since its inception in 1977 (as *Room of One's Own*), the magazine has been run by a volunteer collective of women who believe the publishing landscape needs a space that reflects women's strength, sensuality, vulnerability, and wit. Each issue brings together fiction, interviews, art, poetry, reviews, and essays that form a dialogue on the female experience, with works by writers and artists such as Carol Shields, Joan Givner, Eleanor Wachtel, Susan Point, Nancy Lee, and Frances Itani. Submissions and subscriptions: Box 46160 Stn. D, Vancouver, British Columbia, V6J 5G5. Email: contactus@roommagazine.com Website: www.roommagazine.com

For more than four decades, **This Magazine** has proudly published fiction and poetry from new and emerging Canadian writers. A sassy and thoughtful journal of arts, politics, and pop culture, *This* consistently offers fresh takes on familiar issues, as well as breaking stories that need to be told. Publisher: Lisa Whittington-Hill. Editor: Graham F. Scott. Fiction & Poetry Editor: Stuart Ross. Correspondence: *This Magazine*, Suite 396, 401 Richmond Ave. W., Toronto, Ontario, M5V 3A8. Website: www.this.org

Vancouver Review is an iconoclastic, irreverent, and wholly independent cultural quarterly that focuses on B.C. cultural, social, and political issues, and publishes commentary, essays, and narrative non-fiction, as well as fiction and poetry in every issue. With its Blueprint B.C. Fiction Series, launched in the summer of 2007, *Vancouver Review* explores the zeitgeist and geographic implications of the province through illustrated stories by first-time and established authors. Editor: Gudrun Will. Fiction Editor: Zsuzsi Gartner. Poetry Editor: Caroline Harvey. Submissions and correspondence (email submissions preferred): *Vancouver Review*, 2828 West 13th Avenue, Vancouver, British Columbia, V6K 2T7. Email: editor@vancouverreview.com Website: www.vancouverreview.com

Submissions were also received from the following journals:

Alberta Views
(Calgary, Alta.)
www.albertaviews.ab.ca

The Antigonish Review
(Antigonish, N.S.)
www.antigonishreview.com

carte blanche
(Montreal, Que.)
www.carte-blanche.org

The Claremont Review
(Victoria, B.C.)
www.theclaremontreview.ca

Descant
(Toronto, Ont.)
www.descant.ca

Event
(New Westminster, B.C.)
www.event.douglas.bc.ca

Exile: The Literary Quarterly
(Holstein, Ont.)
www.exilequarterly.com

The Fiddlehead
(Fredericton, N.B.)
www.thefiddlehead.ca

FreeFall
(Calgary, Alta.)
www.freefallmagazine.ca

Geist
(Vancouver, B.C.)
www.geist.com

Grain
(Saskatoon, Sask.)
www.grainmagazine.ca

The Incongruous Quarterly
(Toronto, Ont.)
www.incongruousquarterly.com

Joyland
(Toronto, Ont.)
www.joyland.ca

The Malahat Review
(Victoria, B.C.)
www.malahatreview.ca

Matrix Magazine
(Montreal, Que.)
www.matrixmagazine.org

The Nashwaak Review
(Fredericton, N.B.)
w4.stu.ca/stu/about/publicatio
ns/nashwaak/nashwaak.aspx

The New Quarterly
(Waterloo, Ont.)
www.tnq.ca

Paperplates
(Toronto, Ont.)
www.paperplates.org

The Prairie Journal
(Calgary, Alta.)
www.prairiejournal.org

The Puritan
(Toronto, Ont.)
www.puritan-magazine.com

Queen's Quarterly
(Kingston, Ont.)
www.queensu.ca/quarterly

Riddle Fence
(St. Johns, N.L.)
www.riddlefence.com

subTerrain
(Vancouver, B.C.)
www.subterrain.ca

Taddle Creek
(Toronto, Ont.)
www.taddlecreekmag.com

The Windsor Review
(Windsor, Ont.)
www.windsorreview.wordpress
.com

PREVIOUS CONTRIBUTING AUTHORS

* Winners of the $10,000 Journey Prize
** Co-winners of the $10,000 Journey Prize

1

1989

SELECTED WITH ALISTAIR MACLEOD

Ven Begamudré, "Word Games"
David Bergen, "Where You're From"
Lois Braun, "The Pumpkin-Eaters"
Constance Buchanan, "Man with Flying Genitals"
Ann Copeland, "Obedience"
Marion Douglas, "Flags"
Frances Itani, "An Evening in the Café"
Diane Keating, "The Crying Out"
Thomas King, "One Good Story, That One"
Holley Rubinsky, "Rapid Transits"*
Jean Rysstad, "Winter Baby"
Kevin Van Tighem, "Whoopers"
M.G. Vassanji, "In the Quiet of a Sunday Afternoon"
Bronwen Wallace, "Chicken 'N' Ribs"
Armin Wiebe, "Mouse Lake"
Budge Wilson, "Waiting"

2

1990

SELECTED WITH LEON ROOKE; GUY VANDERHAEGHE

André Alexis, "Despair: Five Stories of Ottawa"

Glen Allen, "The Hua Guofeng Memorial Warehouse"

Marusia Bociurkiw, "Mama, Donya"

Virgil Burnett, "Billfrith the Dreamer"

Margaret Dyment, "Sacred Trust"

Cynthia Flood, "My Father Took a Cake to France"*

Douglas Glover, "Story Carved in Stone"

Terry Griggs, "Man with the Axe"

Rick Hillis, "Limbo River"

Thomas King, "The Dog I Wish I Had, I Would Call It Helen"

K.D. Miller, "Sunrise Till Dark"

Jennifer Mitton, "Let Them Say"

Lawrence O'Toole, "Goin' to Town with Katie Ann"

Kenneth Radu, "A Change of Heart"

Jenifer Sutherland, "Table Talk"

Wayne Tefs, "Red Rock and After"

3

1991

SELECTED WITH JANE URQUHART

Donald Aker, "The Invitation"

Anton Baer, "Yukon"

Allan Barr, "A Visit from Lloyd"

David Bergen, "The Fall"

Rai Berzins, "Common Sense"

Diana Hartog, "Theories of Grief"

Diane Keating, "The Salem Letters"

Yann Martel, "The Facts Behind the Helsinki Roccamatios"*

Jennifer Mitton, "Polaroid"

Sheldon Oberman, "This Business with Elijah"

Lynn Podgurny, "Till Tomorrow, Maple Leaf Mills"

James Riseborough, "She Is Not His Mother"

Patricia Stone, "Living on the Lake"

4
1992
SELECTED WITH SANDRA BIRDSELL

David Bergen, "The Bottom of the Glass"

Maria A. Billion, "No Miracles Sweet Jesus"

Judith Cowan, "By the Big River"

Steven Heighton, "A Man Away from Home Has No Neighbours"

Steven Heighton, "How Beautiful upon the Mountains"

L. Rex Kay, "Travelling"

Rozena Maart, "No Rosa, No District Six"*

Guy Malet De Carteret, "Rainy Day"

Carmelita McGrath, "Silence"

Michael Mirolla, "A Theory of Discontinuous Existence"

Diane Juttner Perreault, "Bella's Story"

Eden Robinson, "Traplines"

5
1993
SELECTED WITH GUY VANDERHAEGHE

Caroline Adderson, "Oil and Dread"

David Bergen, "La Rue Prevette"

Marina Endicott, "With the Band"

Dayv James-French, "Cervine"

Michael Kenyon, "Durable Tumblers"
K.D. Miller, "A Litany in Time of Plague"
Robert Mullen, "Flotsam"
Gayla Reid, "Sister Doyle's Men"*
Oakland Ross, "Bang-bang"
Robert Sherrin, "Technical Battle for Trial Machine"
Carol Windley, "The Etruscans"

6

1994

SELECTED WITH DOUGLAS GLOVER; JUDITH CHANT (CHAPTERS)

Anne Carson, "Water Margins: An Essay on Swimming by My Brother"
Richard Cumyn, "The Sound He Made"
Genni Gunn, "Versions"
Melissa Hardy, "Long Man the River"*
Robert Mullen, "Anomie"
Vivian Payne, "Free Falls"
Jim Reil, "Dry"
Robyn Sarah, "Accept My Story"
Joan Skogan, "Landfall"
Dorothy Speak, "Relatives in Florida"
Alison Wearing, "Notes from Under Water"

7

1995

SELECTED WITH M.G. VASSANJI;
RICHARD BACHMANN (A DIFFERENT DRUMMER BOOKS)

Michelle Alfano, "Opera"
Mary Borsky, "Maps of the Known World"
Gabriella Goliger, "Song of Ascent"

Elizabeth Hay, "Hand Games"

Shaena Lambert, "The Falling Woman"

Elise Levine, "Boy"

Roger Burford Mason, "The Rat-Catcher's Kiss"

Antanas Sileika, "Going Native"

Kathryn Woodward, "Of Marranos and Gilded Angels"*

8

1996

SELECTED WITH OLIVE SENIOR;

BEN MCNALLY (NICHOLAS HOARE LTD.)

Rick Bowers, "Dental Bytes"

David Elias, "How I Crossed Over"

Elyse Gasco, "Can You Wave Bye Bye, Baby?"*

Danuta Gleed, "Bones"

Elizabeth Hay, "The Friend"

Linda Holeman, "Turning the Worm"

Elaine Littman, "The Winner's Circle"

Murray Logan, "Steam"

Rick Maddocks, "Lessons from the Sputnik Diner"

K.D. Miller, "Egypt Land"

Gregor Robinson, "Monster Gaps"

Alma Subasic, "Dust"

9

1997

SELECTED WITH NINO RICCI; NICHOLAS PASHLEY

(UNIVERSITY OF TORONTO BOOKSTORE)

Brian Bartlett, "Thomas, Naked"

Dennis Bock, "Olympia"

Kristen den Hartog, "Wave"
Gabriella Goliger, "Maladies of the Inner Ear"**
Terry Griggs, "Momma Had a Baby"
Mark Anthony Jarman, "Righteous Speedboat"
Judith Kalman, "Not for Me a Crown of Thorns"
Andrew Mullins, "The World of Science"
Sasenarine Persaud, "Canada Geese and Apple Chatney"
Anne Simpson, "Dreaming Snow"**
Sarah Withrow, "Ollie"
Terence Young, "The Berlin Wall"

10

1998

SELECTED BY PETER BUITENHUIS; HOLLEY RUBINSKY; CELIA DUTHIE (DUTHIE BOOKS LTD.)

John Brooke, "The Finer Points of Apples"*
Ian Colford, "The Reason for the Dream"
Libby Creelman, "Cruelty"
Michael Crummey, "Serendipity"
Stephen Guppy, "Downwind"
Jane Eaton Hamilton, "Graduation"
Elise Levine, "You Are You Because Your Little Dog Loves You"
Jean McNeil, "Bethlehem"
Liz Moore, "Eight-Day Clock"
Edward O'Connor, "The Beatrice of Victoria College"
Tim Rogers, "Scars and Other Presents"
Denise Ryan, "Marginals, Vivisections, and Dreams"
Madeleine Thien, "Simple Recipes"
Cheryl Tibbetts, "Flowers of Africville"

11

1999

SELECTED BY LESLEY CHOYCE; SHELDON CURRIE;

MARY-JO ANDERSON (FROG HOLLOW BOOKS)

Mike Barnes, "In Florida"

Libby Creelman, "Sunken Island"

Mike Finigan, "Passion Sunday"

Jane Eaton Hamilton, "Territory"

Mark Anthony Jarman, "Travels into Several Remote Nations of the World"

Barbara Lambert, "Where the Bodies Are Kept"

Linda Little, "The Still"

Larry Lynch, "The Sitter"

Sandra Sabatini, "The One With the News"

Sharon Steams, "Brothers"

Mary Walters, "Show Jumping"

Alissa York, "The Back of the Bear's Mouth"*

12

2000

SELECTED BY CATHERINE BUSH; HAL NIEDZVIECKI;

MARC GLASSMAN (PAGES BOOKS AND MAGAZINES)

Andrew Gray, "The Heart of the Land"

Lee Henderson, "Sheep Dub"

Jessica Johnson, "We Move Slowly"

John Lavery, "The Premier's New Pyjamas"

J.A. McCormack, "Hearsay"

Nancy Richler, "Your Mouth Is Lovely"

Andrew Smith, "Sightseeing"

Karen Solie, "Onion Calendar"

Timothy Taylor, "Doves of Townsend"*

Timothy Taylor, "Pope's Own"

Timothy Taylor, "Silent Cruise"

R.M. Vaughan, "Swan Street"

13

2001

SELECTED BY ELYSE GASCO; MICHAEL HELM;

MICHAEL NICHOLSON (INDIGO BOOKS & MUSIC INC.)

Kevin Armstrong, "The Cane Field"*

Mike Barnes, "Karaoke Mon Amour"

Heather Birrell, "Machaya"

Heather Birrell, "The Present Perfect"

Craig Boyko, "The Gun"

Vivette J. Kady, "Anything That Wiggles"

Billie Livingston, "You're Taking All the Fun Out of It"

Annabel Lyon, "Fishes"

Lisa Moore, "The Way the Light Is"

Heather O'Neill, "Little Suitcase"

Susan Rendell, "In the Chambers of the Sea"

Tim Rogers, "Watch"

Margrith Schraner, "Dream Dig"

14

2002

SELECTED BY ANDRÉ ALEXIS;

DEREK McCORMACK; DIANE SCHOEMPERLEN

Mike Barnes, "Cogagwee"

Geoffrey Brown, "Listen"

Jocelyn Brown, "Miss Canada"*

Emma Donoghue, "What Remains"

Jonathan Goldstein, "You Are a Spaceman With Your Head Under the Bathroom Stall Door"

Robert McGill, "Confidence Men"

Robert McGill, "The Stars Are Falling"

Nick Melling, "Philemon"

Robert Mullen, "Alex the God"

Karen Munro, "The Pool"

Leah Postman, "Being Famous"

Neil Smith, "Green Fluorescent Protein"

15

2003

SELECTED BY MICHELLE BERRY;

TIMOTHY TAYLOR; MICHAEL WINTER

Rosaria Campbell, "Reaching"

Hilary Dean, "The Lemon Stories"

Dawn Rae Downton, "Hansel and Gretel"

Anne Fleming, "Gay Dwarves of America"

Elyse Friedman, "Truth"

Charlotte Gill, "Hush"

Jessica Grant, "My Husband's Jump"*

Jacqueline Honnet, "Conversion Classes"

S.K. Johannesen, "Resurrection"

Avner Mandelman, "Cuckoo"

Tim Mitchell, "Night Finds Us"

Heather O'Neill, "The Difference Between Me and Goldstein"

16

2004

SELECTED BY ELIZABETH HAY; LISA MOORE; MICHAEL REDHILL

Anar Ali, "Baby Khaki's Wings"

Kenneth Bonert, "Packers and Movers"

Jennifer Clouter, "Benny and the Jets"

Daniel Griffin, "Mercedes Buyer's Guide"

Michael Kissinger, "Invest in the North"

Devin Krukoff, "The Last Spark"*

Elaine McCluskey, "The Watermelon Social"

William Metcalfe, "Nice Big Car, Rap Music Coming Out the Window"

Lesley Millard, "The Uses of the Neckerchief"

Adam Lewis Schroeder, "Burning the Cattle at Both Ends"

Michael V. Smith, "What We Wanted"

Neil Smith, "Isolettes"

Patricia Rose Young, "Up the Clyde on a Bike"

17

2005

SELECTED BY JAMES GRAINGER AND NANCY LEE

Randy Boyagoda, "Rice and Curry Yacht Club"

Krista Bridge, "A Matter of Firsts"

Josh Byer, "Rats, Homosex, Saunas, and Simon"

Craig Davidson, "Failure to Thrive"

McKinley M. Hellenes, "Brighter Thread"

Catherine Kidd, "Green-Eyed Beans"

Pasha Malla, "The Past Composed"

Edward O'Connor, "Heard Melodies Are Sweet"

Barbara Romanik, "Seven Ways into Chandigarh"

Sandra Sabatini, "The Dolphins at Sainte Marie"

Matt Shaw, "Matchbook for a Mother's Hair"*

Richard Simas, "Anthropologies"

Neil Smith, "Scrapbook"

Emily White, "Various Metals"

18

2006

SELECTED BY STEVEN GALLOWAY;

ZSUZSI GARTNER; ANNABEL LYON

Heather Birrell, "BriannaSusannaAlana"*

Craig Boyko, "The Baby"

Craig Boyko, "The Beloved Departed"

Nadia Bozak, "Heavy Metal Housekeeping"

Lee Henderson, "Conjugation"

Melanie Little, "Wrestling"

Matthew Rader, "The Lonesome Death of Joseph Fey"

Scott Randall, "Law School"

Sarah Selecky, "Throwing Cotton"

Damian Tarnopolsky, "Sleepy"

Martin West, "Cretacea"

David Whitton, "The Eclipse"

Clea Young, "Split"

19

2007

SELECTED BY CAROLINE ADDERSON;

DAVID BEZMOZGIS; DIONNE BRAND

Andrew J. Borkowski, "Twelve Versions of Lech"

Craig Boyko, "OZY"*

Grant Buday, "The Curve of the Earth"

Nicole Dixon, "High-water Mark"

Krista Foss, "Swimming in Zanzibar"

Pasha Malla, "Respite"

Alice Petersen, "After Summer"

Patricia Robertson, "My Hungarian Sister"

Rebecca Rosenblum, "Chilly Girl"

Nicholas Ruddock, "How Eunice Got Her Baby"

Jean Van Loon, "Stardust"

20

2008

SELECTED BY LYNN COADY; HEATHER O'NEILL; NEIL SMITH

Théodora Armstrong, "Whale Stories"

Mike Christie, "Goodbye Porkpie Hat"

Anna Leventhal, "The Polar Bear at the Museum"

Naomi K. Lewis, "The Guiding Light"

Oscar Martens, "Breaking on the Wheel"

Dana Mills, "Steaming for Godthab"

Saleema Nawaz, "My Three Girls"*

Scott Randall, "The Gifted Class"

S. Kennedy Sobol, "Some Light Down"

Sarah Steinberg, "At Last at Sea"

Clea Young, "Chaperone"

21

2009

SELECTED BY CAMILLA GIBB;
LEE HENDERSON; REBECCA ROSENBLUM

Daniel Griffin, "The Last Great Works of Alvin Cale"

Jesus Hardwell, "Easy Living"

Paul Headrick, "Highlife"
Sarah Keevil, "Pyro"
Adrian Michael Kelly, "Lure"
Fran Kimmel, "Picturing God's Ocean"
Lynne Kutsukake, "Away"
Alexander MacLeod, "Miracle Mile"
Dave Margoshes, "The Wisdom of Solomon"
Shawn Syms, "On the Line"
Sarah L. Taggart, "Deaf"
Yasuko Thanh, "Floating Like the Dead"*

22

2010

SELECTED BY PASHA MALLA; JOAN THOMAS; ALISSA YORK

Carolyn Black, "Serial Love"
Andrew Boden, "Confluence of Spoors"
Laura Boudreau, "The Dead Dad Game"
Devon Code, "Uncle Oscar"*
Danielle Egan, "Publicity"
Krista Foss, "The Longitude of Okay"
Lynne Kutsukake, "Mating"
Ben Lof, "When in the Field with Her at His Back"
Andrew MacDonald, "Eat Fist!"
Eliza Robertson, "Ship's Log"
Mike Spry, "Five Pounds Short and Apologies to Nelson Algren"
Damian Tarnopolsky, "Laud We the Gods"